Do Not Open

Fifteen Tales of Horror

by
Michael Gore

www.DarkInkBooks.com

Do Not Open was first published in *P is for Poltergeist* by Red Cape Publishing 2023

Tracks was first published in *Railroad Tales* by Midnight Street Press 2021

Thanks for Answering was first published in *It Calls From Doors* by Eerie River 2021

Eighteen Letters was first published in *Executive Dread* by Jolly Horror 2021

Likes was first published in *Consumed* by Denver Horror Collective 2020

The Vestige was first published in *I Cast You Out!* By Pulp Cult 2022

A Happy Story was first published in *White Ash* by Dark Ink Books 2009

First Published by Dark Ink Books, Southwick, MA, 2023

Dark Ink and its logos are trademarked by *AM Ink Publishing*.

www.AMInkPublishing.com

For the great horror author, Rebecca Rowland.
Thank you for having a darker mind than mine.
And for always pushing me to write.

Contents

Do Not Open

The wake was awful; the funeral was beyond devastating. Losing her dad was something Tia never wanted to imagine, and yet here she was sitting alone in the back of a beat-up limo on the way to the fourteen-dollar-a-person funeral reception. She hated how much the caterer wanted and spent over half an hour arguing with them and negotiating a price, each time removing an item to make the cost more palatable. In the end, it went from a high-end lunch with Beef Wellington at twenty-four dollars to a simple chicken and fish option ten dollars lower. Saving ten dollars a head was the best feeling Tia has had since her dad had died, especially since he was always so cheap and would have been proud of her negotiation skills. In the end, though, it was a sliver of solace in her ocean of pain.

At fifty-one, having two ex-husbands and one venomous child who left for college ten years ago and never looked back, her father was the only consistent thing in her life and now he was gone. For over thirty years, Dad smoked a pack a day, sometimes two, drank a thirty-pack of the cheapest beer he could find every week, and ate more processed meats in a single sitting than any human should in a month. Death should have called him years earlier, and yet the heart attack that took him in his sleep at seventy-four was the most shocking thing Tia had ever experienced, more than when her mother died of suicide when she was nine.

Mom had been gone so long she didn't think of her much, but when she did, she always heard the line, *I'm going to get bread for dinner, Tia, I'll be right back,* ring in her head. Mom never got bread; instead, she stopped her car in the middle of the bridge and jumped into the Connecticut River. She would have lived if she hadn't weighed herself down with ankle weights and rocks in all her pockets. It was planned, and yet she said she would be right back. Tia had deep personal issues with the trauma, which both husbands blamed for the divorces, but Tia disagreed and said she'd grown up good and "normal" because her dad stepped up and took care of her better than two parents could have. The day Dad told her that her mother died, he got down on both knees so he could look her in the eyes and said not to worry, that she would never be alone and that he would always be there for her—and he was, until now.

Dad was her constant, the only consistent person in her life that she could always call, run to, or depend on for absolutely anything. From boy trouble in her teens to a DUI in college to the divorces, Dad was there with a big hug, an arm around her shoulder, sage advice, and even financial or physical help when needed. Alone in the back of that limo, her mind raced with all the times he was there and all the comforting things he did, from ice cream parties to cheer her up to flying to Italy to comfort her when her new semester-abroad "boyfriend" left her stranded in an ocean villa with an astronomical bill. Even just last week, Dad had shown up unannounced on a Thursday night with two pints of ice cream. Like always, he let her pick which flavor she wanted, mint chocolate chip, and the movie they watched as they savored every scoop of the creamy goodness. *God, I loved him,* Tia thought to herself before breaking down in heavy and uncontrollable sobs for the first time.

It took Tia almost an entire week after the funeral to get the nerve to enter her dad's home, which of course she was set to inherit along with everything he had. Dad was a blue-collar worker with an average ranch home, but with everything combined, it would let her retire a few years early, which made her smile as that was her dad: looking out for her one last time. It was her childhood house and she felt more at home there than in her own. Walking in for the first time without her dad being inside waiting for her with a warm hug was like entering an empty Disney World with all the rides and lights off and the characters gone forever; the happiest place on earth no more. Sliding the door open, smelling that all-too-familiar smell, which she could never place but just called it "Dad smell," made her heart throb with longing for one more hug. She had cried enough for a lifetime in the past week, yet a few more tears spilled out of her eyes as she looked around the room, taking in how quiet and still it was.

After walking around smelling and touching things like she was in a sappy Lifetime movie, Tia made her way to the refrigerator, knowing she had to clean that out first. It was an odd task and hard seeing the things her Dad had put away to finish or planned to eat that week, but no matter what it was, it went into the big black trash bags and then right into the bins outside. With that task done, she sat at the kitchen table and took a break while sipping on the one Pepsi she saved for herself. The memories from decades in that kitchen were all there fighting for her attention, but she'd had enough of playing memory lane and pushed them aside to think of the "business aspect of death."

Normally, anything to do with any big decisions or business issues, Dad would be the first call; then he'd be there to help her make the decision or at least for support. Now she was completely alone. This weighed on her heavily, but she knew if Dad was looking down on her, he would want her to pick her head up and do the work. While she'd decided to have an auction company come and sell off the contents and the house, she still had to go through every room to take anything she wanted and to find any important paperwork. *Well, if you want to find paperwork, the obvious place to start is the office, sweetheart.* The voice of her dad was soft in her head; it made her smile, even though she knew it was her own thoughts.

Dad's office, which was the smallest of the three bedrooms in the house, was a place she had been in many times, though she'd never spent more than a few moments in the memorabilia-filled room. The walls were covered in pictures, ninety percent of which were of her at various stages in her life. There were some news articles, framed records, and of course, Dad's "Beers of the World" collection that rimmed the top of the room on a wooden shelf. Dad had always prided himself on the collection and showed any visitor the bottles he got and drank from around the world. Tia felt a bit of sadness creep in when she realized that something her Dad treasured so much would simply be recycled soon. *One man's treasure is another's trash.* Ignoring this revelation, she sat at the desk and started her work.

An hour in, she had gone through everything on top of the desk, including the stacks of unfiled bills and nick-knacks that Tia wondered why Dad kept. It was weird seeing the inside of Dad's drawers. She was so close to him and came to his house every week, yet the things inside his drawers were a mystery to her. Why did he keep four smooth and ugly rocks? Why did he have an entire drawer full of enough pens and rulers to supply a school? Why was one drawer absolutely empty when every other one was filled with various junk? Tia started to realize you could know someone deeply, but never completely.

The only drawer left was the bottom right; it was the same size as the two drawers above it and Tia expected to just find more "desk"-type things. As she reached for it, with no warning, one of Dad's prized bottles, a green one with a bright yellow sticker of an orange sun, fell off the shelf and shattered right behind Tia. Having not worked out since her high school gym class and having eaten a steady diet of Dad's bonding ice cream for the past twenty years, Tia's chest tightened and a million tiny needles flew into her heart as if thrown by an invisible tribe of angry warriors. The lack of breathing and the chest pain scared her more than the bottle had. It was so bad she ran out of the room and to the kitchen to grab her cell phone to call for help, but by the time she had it in her hands, the tiny darts fell out and she was catching her breath. After five minutes of slow breathing and a dozen sips of soda, Tia made her way back to the room with a dustpan and broom. It wasn't until she was kneeling and picking up the shards did she start to wonder how the hell the thing fell.

Tia was upset the bottle broke, knowing Dad would have been devastated to lose one, but at the same time, she knew all their fate would be similar; no one was going to want dusty old empty beer bottles. *But how did it fall?* Reminding herself that she is an atheist and didn't believe in ghosts, she let go of the incident and sat back down at the desk after throwing the shards away. Reaching for that last drawer once more, she felt her heart start to speed up. She tensed, waiting for another bottle to fall, but nothing happened when she slid the drawer out. Inside the dark wood of the drawer was a black lock box that fit snuggly inside, taking up every ounce of space. This was curious to Tia, as she had already found Dad's "important" documents like his passport, will, credit cards, and such. *What would Dad lock in here?* A queasy feeling of fear and excitement started to flow through her body.

Tia had to use a letter opener to lift the box up enough for her to grab it out, as she couldn't get her fingers around it. With it on top of the desk in front of her, seeing the words etched into the side, the excitement of it possibly being money Dad hid vanished. Carved into the side of the box, deep into the black paint with crude letters, was:

DO NOT OPEN. Destroy. – Dad

Tia swallowed hard as her mind raced, wondering what could be inside. *Love letters? Sex toys? A gun?* She always listened to her dad, took his advice as the law, and always, always respected what he asked. He was just too damn good to her not to. Disappointing him was the worst thing she could ever think of doing. Yet, she knew from the second she found the box that she would be opening it. Part of her wanted to sit and pretend to debate what to do so she could feel better about her decision, but it was pointless. Grabbing the metal letter opener, which reminded her more of a fancy knife to kill someone you loved with, rather than something to open paper with, she jammed it between the crack of the lid. The metal scratching sound was like demons screaming in her ear. After several metallic screams, she realized the demons were telling her that the key had to be in the damn house.

Two minutes later, she had the small silver key in her hand; it was right there on his key chain, next to his shed key, sitting there inconspicuously all these years. *The key was in plain sight and the box just in a drawer; it can't be all that bad,* Tia thought as she stuck the tiny key into the lock. Lifting the lid, her mind went blank with confusion at the site of four neat and organized rows of MiniDV tapes. She hadn't seen those old camcorder tapes in years, and yet here were dozens of them, each one labeled with a date and two initials afterwards. Tia could not fathom what was on them and why her father would have locked them up with a warning to throw them out. Her stomach rolled as if it were falling uncontrollably down a steep hill.

Tia didn't have a single memory of her dad having a video camera; in fact, she was positive he didn't. There were no childhood videos of her—*none*. Dad always just had a cheap film camera he used on vacations, never a video camera. Picking up one tape, she looked at it: *4/24/92 – J.M.* Tia assumed it was a year and maybe…someone's initials? While Tia hadn't had sex in almost a decade, she wasn't a prude; she understood that these could be sex tapes her dad had made. The idea repulsed her, but it also didn't make sense. Dad had never had a girlfriend, not once in her entire life. When she was older, she even tried to set him up, but he'd refused. The curiosity was starting to boil over.

After a quick internet search, she found out that she had to have a MiniDV camcorder attached to the television through wires to watch the video. *If Dad had all of these, then he had to have a camera. How else would he watch them…or make the tapes for that matter?* It took Tia over an hour of searching through closets, drawers, and boxes before she found the camera, and when she did, her gut sank. Dad had a camera alright; it was in his underwear drawer, right under the television in his bedroom. The part that made her sick was that her dad had drilled a hole in the back of the dresser so the wires could come out the back and into the television. Whatever was on the tapes, Dad had watched enough to drill a hole so it could always stay set up.

Throw them away, baby girl. Come on, throw them away and get back to work. The voice sounded so clear in her head: her dad, her loving dad, warning, pleading with her, yet she ignored it and took the tape from April of '92 to Dad's room, powered on the television, popped in the tape, and sat on the bed. Switching over to the correct input, a bright blue fuzziness filled the screen. *Stop it, stop it. Throw them all way.* The words boomed in the room *out loud.* Tia jumped up and felt those tiny darts in her heart again as she looked around the room in a panic. It was her dad's voice, clear as day, but angrier and louder than she had ever heard it. Shaking off the darts, she told herself she was hearing things, that it was part of the grief process, and turned to the screen that was flickering. Wavy lines jumped and scrolled until they finally settled onto a shot of what she recognized as her dad's dank and dirty basement wall. There was a metal chair and nothing else in the shot. The image sat there still, scuffling noises in the background. When a young man, maybe mid-twenties, shuffled into the shot, his mouth gagged, his hands tied, Tia let out an audible gasp.

While it would still destroy every image and understanding she had of her father, she prayed that her dad was into some sort of weird BDSM. She was not that lucky. With the man sitting in the chair, it looked like some sort of grainy hostage video. What she didn't understand was why the man willingly and calmly sat down. Did her dad have a gun pointed at him? Was it some sort of role play? After a few seconds, the camera zoomed in a bit on the man, filling the screen with his head and shoulders. Suddenly, the light started to flicker in the basement and she could hear her dad's voice, the voice she missed so much.

"Please accept this sacrifice we give to you." Tia was feeling sick as she watched the man start to squirm nervously. A few seconds later, a man walked behind the guy in the chair. When the knife appeared in her dad's hand—and it *was* his hand; he'd always had that misshapen mole at the bottom of his thumb she used to call his smooshed raisin—Tia closed her eyes. The words her dad had said didn't penetrate her mind as she squeezed them shut tighter than she ever had. The only thing she could hear was the wet sawing sound, followed by the sick gurgling noise and the eventual thud. Tia didn't even open her eyes when she fell off the bed onto her knees and vomited into her dad's flower-print mini trashcan.

Wiping her mouth with her sleeve, she opened her eyes and sucked in fresh air, trying to grasp a tiny bit of sanity as her world crashed around her. She had to shut the video off. Getting up, she stumbled towards the television, but froze when she saw the screen. The camera had pulled back out; it showed more of the basement than before. The man's body was on the floor, a lake of blood forming around his head and shoulders, but that was to be expected. What wasn't expected was seeing her twenty-something-year-old self on the screen, standing next to her dad who was cleaning his bloody hands.

"Why do you always get to cut them, Dad?" she heard her younger self say in a whiny, coy voice she had never used in her life.

"You know why, honey. If you do it, you'll never be free. This is my responsibility." Tia was frozen in disbelief. She had to be having a mental break because what she was seeing was utterly impossible. *Dad could never hurt a fly, let alone kill people, and I would, I would never...* Tia's brain was on overload. She wanted it all to stop; she wished she had heeded the warning and thrown the damned box away.

"You ready to eat, sweetheart?" the man, who she could no longer think of as her dad, asked on the screen. Tia whispered, "No," just as her younger self giddily exclaimed that she was. Tia ripped the camcorder out of the drawer and threw it on the bed, killing the awful video feed.

Tia drank half a bottle of bourbon; it burned like hell fire and made her want to puke again, yet it did nothing to calm her nerves. Sitting in the kitchen, the house silent, she racked her brain, trying to figure out how what she saw could be real. She didn't have the tiniest of memories of anything in that video, not even a vague *déjà vu*. How could she have no memories of her father murdering a man in front of her? *Wait, there had to be three dozen tapes. Was that randomly the only one I was in? The only murder?* The thought made the bourbon start to bubble up in her throat. Mathematically, the odds of her pulling out the only video of her were... *Why do you always get to cut them, Daddy?* She had to be in the others.

Hooking the camera back up, setting the black box and all the evil little tapes next to her, she felt like she was prepping her own execution, but she had to know, she had to understand how her perfect dad could have done such things. *Start from the beginning,* she heard her dad's voice say in her head as she grabbed the very first tape, labeled *9/13/74.* The second she put the tape in and pushed play, she jumped at the sound of another bottle falling off from its high perch and shattering on the floor. Hearing the shards skitter to a rest, she knew something deeper was going on than she could fathom.

The second this video started to play, she could tell it was a transfer of an old Super 8 film. There was no sound and the image was so grainy it was hard to tell what it was until her four-year-old head came into focus. Her tiny, smiling face looked happy as she waved to the camera. It made Tia grin and feel warm before she realized that the video was going to turn dark very soon. Within seconds, the tiny Tia stopped smiling, stopped waving, and looked dead into the camera. Her small mouth started to say something. Tia couldn't read the lips, but she could tell they were the same words over and over. Then a tiny trickle of blood leaked out of her left eye, like a lone red tear, leaving a snail trail of deep red down her cheek. Seconds later, the camera lens cracked.

Tia didn't understand anything she was seeing. The image of her was followed by a cut, the crack now gone, and a shot of a man talking to her young father in a kitchen, tiny Tia sitting in the background playing with dolls. They started to argue. Little Tia noticed, stood up, and then the man just dropped to the floor, his head slamming so hard onto the yellow, paisley-patterned linoleum floor it had to have fractured. The film cut. This was not an answer; it was more confusion.

One by one, Tia put in the tapes. *Every* time she hit play, a bottle fell off the shelf and shattered, as if an imaginary string were connected from the play button to each one. Video after video, she grew more confused. The killing didn't start until the fourth one. Of course, young Tia was right there next to her dad, who looked terrified the first time he sliced a neck. As the videos went on, he got more and more confident until he seemed to truly enjoy the gruesome task. Tia herself grew from a mere toddler to the ripe old age of nine when her mother made a cameo appearance in one of the films. There was screaming and crying and it ended with her dad holding her mom down in a puddle of blood to stop her from flailing her arms. Little Tia herself skipped to the camera to shut it off while the ordeal happened. When she looked at the date on the box, she was not surprised that it was the day before Mom's suicide. *I should not have opened the box.*

Tia had no clue what time it was when she got down to the last video. The sun had disappeared and blackness had taken over the room ages ago, leaving her sitting in nothing but the flickering blue light of murder. Even though she had no clue how many bottles her dad had in his office, she knew at that moment there was only one left on the shelf as she popped in the last tape. The shattering sound seemed to echo louder this time. The video's date was the same as the day her dad died. While disgusted and broken, part of her felt sad that it was the last video of her dad she would get to see. When the screen came on, just like the other videos, she saw the basement and the chair. This time, though, it was her dad sitting in the chair, sitting and staring at the camera with sad eyes. Then she saw herself walk into frame. Ironically, she was wearing the same dingy gray "Bahamas or Bust" shirt she had on now. Two weeks ago, Tia looked sad, just like her dad.

"Are you sure about this, Dad?" The audio on the screen was subtle and hard to hear, but Tia suddenly did not need to hear it. She remembered her dad's words; she remembered the feel of his life going out of his body and how absolutely crushing it was. *Remember, put the tape in the box, bring it to the safety deposit box, then throw the key in the river. You have to do it fast; the bank is only open another few hours. You cannot go tomorrow. You won't remember and if you find the box after that...no one can help you. I made it think it was me all these years, and when I die, it might be fooled; it might move on. If you don't do this and you find the tapes and a single memory comes back...oh God, oh baby, please, please promise me you'll lock them away. I've worked so hard to make your life good. I don't want it ruined now.*

Tia's mouth was dry. She could feel something in her brain start to fire and feel hazy and funny. In a way it felt like there was a massive, pressurized container deep underwater that was about to explode in her head and poison everything.

I kept it away as long as I could. I hope this time it will be forever. This was all for you. Her dad sobbed on the screen. Tia closed her eyes as she heard the last line, not wanting to see how she was about to induce a heart attack. *Why didn't she listen? The one time she didn't listen…*

Just as the video went to static, the room suddenly filled with a dense humidity, as if steam-room jets started blasting. Her skin moistened from the dampness and static electricity started to dance up and down her arms as she felt the thing enter the room and stand behind her. When the metallic baritone voice said her name in a booming whisper, she whipped a tear from her eye and saw that it was blood. Looking down at the three words etched into the metal box, *Do Not Open*, Tia took a deep breath as she prepared to take over her dad's role.

Thanks for Answering

The day they put it in, half the darn street came to see it. They all looked at it, gob smacked, and slapped Pa's back, laughing as they held the pepper-shaker-sized thing to their ears.

She couldn't understand why Pa was so darn excited to have that…thing…in their kitchen. Even though there were seven adults all chortling and trying the new phone, making the kitchen feel tiny, Josie felt alone, very alone. She always felt alone. She was the only kid on the street, after all. The girls at school either didn't like her or lived too far away to play with.

A big set of gruff hands pushed her towards the phone. Everyone suddenly looked at her with giddy anticipation, and before she could protest, Pa took the receiver and put it to her ear. The black-painted brass was warm, and it felt sticky and gross.

Who would want to push something against their ear like this? It's like a wet willy, she thought as Pa urged her to speak into the part that looked like the horn on their record player.

"Speak!"

"Say something!"

"Talk, Josie."

"Just say hi, for cherry's sake!"

"Anything would do. Just talk, and you'll hear

them talk back."

"Oh, don't press her. She is scared."

"Kid don't understand how gal darn astounding this is."

"Talk, Josie. Talk!"

"Speak."

"Speak!"

The words slammed at her from every which way. She had no clue who was saying what or why they were being so bossy, but everyone yelling at her made her face hot and tied her tongue.

It was almost impossible, but after the twelfth cajole, she eked out a tiny, shallow, "Hello."

Seconds later, Josie was on the porch, bent over Pa's knee, stockings and underwear pulled to her shoes, her buttocks exposed for everyone to gawk at.

And they gawked, alright. All seven of them came out to watch her get punished—every last one of them.

Whack, whack, whack.

The spankings always hurt, but that time Pa had a callus on his palm at the base of his pointer finger that was rougher than normal, and she could feel it scratching her skin with each slap.

There were mumblings and angry comments. A few told Pa it was enough. Another spoke up and said it wasn't, that the phone was worth more than Josie's whole damn life.

But all Josie could think of were the words that awful, awful voice had said to her that caused the knee-jerk throwing of the ear piece to the floor.

It was a voice of pure evil.

Deep, gravely, and almost hypnotic. The vibrato made the words quiver into her ear and down to her eardrum like some sort of intelligent snake that knew right where to slither. The words scared her.

Your pa killed your ma.

In Sunday school, she was told stories of Satan and how he could try to trick and entice her, but she never thought they were true, let alone that he would talk directly to her.

No one talked to Josie.

Josie brought Pa his evening drink as he sat reading in his chair, just like any other night. Normally, he would kiss her on the cheek, tell her to wash up and go to bed, which she would. However, that night, Pa did not kiss her.

As she started to walk away, he barked, "If that phone stops working, you will have to work off the damage you caused to it."

Josie stood with her back to him. She nodded but waited to be dismissed.

"Josie, I've never been so embarrassed in my life. If there was no company…it wouldn't have been your behind."

Josie sucked in a big breath and dared a response. She burned to tell someone what she'd heard, but she knew they would not believe a child.

"The voice, Pa. The voice scared me, and it said mean and untrue things." With her back still to him, she absent-mindedly touched the raw skin on her behind.

"It was the operator asking you who you wanted to be connected to. That is how the phone works. You pick it up and tell the dame who you want to talk to, and she connects you. You can ask her the time, too. That's who you talked to."

Josie wanted to turn and run to him, to bury her face in his chest and tell him what she really heard, just like Ma would have allowed her to do, but she knew Pa would not tolerate that. So, she nodded and headed to bed. Unfortunately, she had to pass through the kitchen, right by that damn phone.

Josie kept her eyes on it as she passed, as if the thing might leap and strangle her with the thick brown cord. It didn't, and she made it to her room successfully, but the damn thing was only ten steps away from her bed.

Sleeping is not going to be easy, she thought as she put on her nightgown and washed her face in the basin.

Sure enough, every time she closed her eyes, she thought of the creepy black phone. In her mind, it would grow in size, the cord turning slimly and pulsing like a birthing cow's umbilical cord. The thought of that cord whipping out like a lasso, grabbing her tight and pulling her towards it, made her sit up and gasp for air.

It wasn't half a second later that the phone's trill bell rang. It sounded like a metallic kitten purring during an angry nightmare.

Two quick tinny purrs.

Josie felt faint but forced herself to jump up and

flip on the light switch. Instead of a flood of light, the bulb popped in a fat electric snap. Josie yelled and pushed her body against the door.

He is coming for me. He wants me.

Puurrrrriiing.

Puurrrrriiing.

Josie had never wanted her mother more.

Puurrrrriiing.

Puurrrrriiing.

The ringing seemed to get louder as she sank to the floor, holding the door shut. Crossing herself, Josie started to pray—fast, hard, and with more conviction than she ever had.

Puurrrrriiing.

Puurrrrriiing.

Yet, it wouldn't stop.

Why isn't Pa waking up? Why doesn't he get the gal darn phone?

Anger started to take over the fear, the ringing making her want to smash the phone into pieces. Over and over, it wouldn't stop. It grew so loud she couldn't hear her own prayers anymore. She had to answer it. She had to tell the voice to leave her alone, or else.

Or else what?

As she stood up, her legs wobbled in a way that made her think of a newborn calf...*and that throbbing umbilical cord*. With a deep breath, she grabbed the handle and pulled the door open, half expecting to see Satan himself standing in the kitchen, holding the phone out to her.

But it was just her kitchen, the phone on the counter the only outlier in the room.

The ringing was so loud she had to cover her ears. There was no way Pa could sleep through it. It was louder than a 'dozer stuck in a mud pit, revving its engines full throttle. After a quick look around the room to be certain there were no demons, Josie locked her eyes on the phone. Despite the noise it was making, it was eerily still.

She stood two feet from the phone—the phone that had caused her such embarrassment and the scratches on her buttocks, not to mention the fright of a lifetime. Josie reached out to the receiver slowly, as if it might bite. The ringing was so deafening she was nervous her ears would start to bleed. The painful cacophony instantly cut to dead silence as she lifted the receiver, the muting so blissful that she silently thanked God.

"Baby J, is that you? Baby J?" It was a voice she had not heard in three years, though she replayed it plenty in her head.

Ma.

She knew it was her, besides the voice being so distinct, because no one else had ever called her Baby J.

"Mama…Mama…how…? Is it really you?" Tears streamed down Josie's face, feelings of joy and relief pouring over her.

"Yes, Baby J. Yes," her ma's voice whispered so wonderfully in her ear.

A second later, Josie spewed out sentence after

sentence of how much she missed her, how she was so scared, what the voice said. But then, she slowed down and asked the important question.

"Ma, how are…where are you?"

There was a long pause, and Josie thought she could hear wind and other whispers in the background.

"Baby J, I'm…in the place you go when you die an unnatural death. I'm stuck here. I can't go to the good place just yet."

Hearing that made Josie's tears of joy turn to sorrow. Ma was dead, and she *wasn't* in Heaven.

"I…I don't understand. You died by accident. Your dress got caught in the hay baler. Wait, how are you talking to me?"

There was a longer pause. Again, she could hear the whispers through the static. "The phone, us, the dead, we have found a way to reach through it. It's almost like a door or a window that we can yell through to be heard."

Josie accepted the explanation and waited for her ma to keep going.

"I-I don't want to tell you this, Baby J, but your pa, he killed me. I can't go to the good place until he pays for what he did with his own life."

Josie felt faint again. Pa was not a loving or kind man, but she never thought he could kill Ma. Then she thought of the anger in the spanking earlier, how he had to be stopped, all the times he did worse to Ma.

"I need you to help me, Baby J. If you don't, I'll be stuck here forever. But worse, when you become a woman, he will do the same things to you that he did to me. We can't let that happen."

Josie felt confused, her stomach twisting and gurgling with fear and a touch of excitement. "Okay." A sudden fear of Pa waking up and walking into the room surged through her.

"See the cord, Baby J? The one attached to the earpiece?"

"Uh huh." Josie didn't want to look at that stinking cord, even if it was bringing her Ma's voice to her ear. She might have been just a "mere pup," as Uncle Carl called her, but she was old enough to understand that she was going to have to do something awful with that cord.

You could just hang up, her mind thought briefly, but Ma was the only one who had ever cared about her. And deep down, Josie knew her death hadn't been an accident.

The night before Ma died, she told Josie to pack a bag and keep it under her bed; they were leaving at first light while Pa was in the field. But when Josie woke, it was already bright. Ma hadn't gotten her up. She was already dead, and Pa had blood on him. He showered and changed before going into town to get help, a detail he told Josie to not tell anyone about ever…or else.

By that night, Pa was playing the role of the grieving father, hugging her in front of the neighbors, kept repeating that Ma was in a *better place*. She was younger then, and she believed him.

Now, though, she believed Ma's voice.

"Go tell your pa that the phone rang. Say the

person said it was important. When he sits to take the call, you need to wrap the cord around his neck. We will do the rest." Her ma's voice was changing slightly. Certain words sounded almost like a reptile, but Josie brushed it off as a bad connection.

"If I do that, you'll go to Heaven, Ma?" Josie asked, picturing her Ma floating up to the heavenly gates she'd learned about in Sunday school.

"If you do that, you will open the door for us, for me, Baby J, and I will be free from this place."

She didn't say Heaven, but Josie knew that was what her ma meant. Ma had to nudge her a few more times, but Josie finally agreed to go get her pa, only because she couldn't take thinking of Ma in a bad place forever.

Josie always hated how the hallway floorboards creaked like they were screaming out in pain when stepped on. As she walked down the hallway to wake her pa, the sound was worse than ever. It was like the boards were shouting to her to stop, to go back to bed, which she desperately wanted, but the image of Ma at the gates of Heaven pushed her past the wailing wood to the open doorway of Pa's bedroom. She licked her lips and took a deep breath as she stared at the large lump under the white comforter that Ma had knitted a few months before she died. Thinking of Ma sitting in her chair, knitting and telling her stories, made Josie angry at Pa for taking her away.

"Pa!" She screamed before even knowing she was

going to. The white blanket shot up in the air, her Pa following behind. "The phone kept ringing. I answered it. They asked for you, said it was important."

Her father was never a pleasant man, but waking him that way, Josie saw that *he* was really the devil, not the voice she heard earlier. Pa screamed and cussed up a storm, then pushed her aside as he stomped down the hall in his pajama bottoms and no shirt. Being pushed against the wall made her already sore buttocks sting, giving her all the motivation she needed to heed Ma's instructions.

She followed Pa into the kitchen, her eyes squinting as he snapped on the lights. Thankfully, Pa did just as Ma said he would; he sat in the chair next to the phone before answering it. Pa put the receiver to his ear and said "Hello" over and over, growing angrier each time.

Josie slipped up next to him and grabbed the candlestick phone, garnering an inquisitive and confused look from her father.

"Josie, if this is some sort of prank, you won't be able to sit for a month!" he barked, growing more confused and annoyed as she quickly raced the phone around him.

Just before he could swat at her, she threw the stick over his shoulder, leaving the cord wrapped around his neck like a lazy scarf.

"Josie!" he screamed, rage dripping from every syllable.

In that moment, Josie feared that she did it wrong,

that it wasn't going to work, that she would get the beating of her life, all while Ma had to suffer in that place forever.

But then it happened.

The cord pulled taut as if invisible hands were tugging it in opposite ways. Her father dropped the receiver and grabbed at his throat. The cord started to quiver, bubble, and grow. It expanded, grew chunky and ropy, just like an umbilical cord.

I knew it, she thought to herself as she backed away.

The light suddenly burst, and the explosion was followed by a loud noise that sounded like a thousand people yawning at once. It came from the phone, growing louder every second. Josie pushed herself against the wall, scared but also proud. Pa's eyes bulged out of his skull in an unnatural way, his face a deep purple; sweat, spit, and snot dripped everywhere. He reached out for her, but the force wouldn't let him move.

It was then that she saw the cord. It was slimy and getting thicker. Somehow, it looked angry. As she stared at it, she noticed it was cutting her father's neck. Blood began to ooze out.

Pa's head suddenly did a small hop up in the air. It paused as his mouth fell slack, then dropped to the floor, blood spraying from his severed neck, pouring, dripping as his hand grasped at nothing before the body fell after its master.

Josie held her breath. She couldn't think, she couldn't move, and she wanted her ma.

When the whispers turned to voices, she got

excited and strained to hear her mother's, but there were so many that she couldn't separate them. She stared at the phone, which was shaking and jumping like popping corn, bouncing in each direction, the umbilical throbbing and growing.

"Ma?" Josie whispered, praying to hear "Baby J" in her ears. Instead, the voices grew to growls and grunts, laughs and cackles, screams and guttural, painful sounds that reminded her of when Pa slaughtered a sow. Then, it all stopped. The phone dropped to the counter and lay still. The umbilical continued to grow bigger and bigger, but the phone still looked normal. Josie took the opportunity to pick up the receiver.

"Ma! Mama!" she yelled into the mouthpiece, the earpiece crammed tight to her head.

She felt a tiny tickle in her ear. She brushed it off like she would a horsefly, but then it turned from a tickle to an actual… *touch*. She pulled the receiver away to look at it, everything inside of her turning to liquid. Reaching out of the small circle was a brown, rotting finger with a broken, jagged fingernail.

Josie threw the phone down and instantly regretted it.

You have to be careful with expensive things, Josie. Pa's words rang in her head as the receiver shattered, freeing whatever was attached to that awful finger.

Josie backed up in horror, tripped over her pa's legs, and fell onto the floor, feeling the sting of her raw bottom. She looked to her left and saw her pa's purple severed head.

"I'm sorry," she whispered as the creatures, one by one, crawled out of the ever-growing cord.

She closed her eyes, hugged her knees, and prayed that one of them would be her ma, but she knew better.

Instead, she heard the raspy, awful voice from earlier.

"Thank you for answering, Josie."

Strings

Everette McDaniel. Freaking Everette McDaniel. Chas couldn't stand still; he moved his legs back and forth so fast he thought his corduroys would catch fire. Since he was ten years old, when he first heard *Cat Run* on the radio while swimming in his aunt's pool one balmy hundred-degree summer day, he has been obsessed with Everette McDaniel. The man was a Rock God. No one could shred a guitar and howl into the microphone the way Everette could, and he was walking right towards Chas. With a deep breath, he did his best to wipe the childish grin off his face, he pushed back his bangs in one cool movement and then flicked his chin up and in a silent gesture that said "hey" as Everette got nearby. When the man he worshiped responded with the same movement, Chas couldn't hold back the smile; it exploded across his face in a goofy and kid-ish manner that was completely embarrassing.

Turning around to keep his eye on the god passing him, hoping he didn't look too stupid, Chas reached down and pinched his leg through the brown pants to be sure he wasn't dreaming. Being a roadie was going to be bad ass. Not only was he going to get to hear Everett play every night, but he was also going to be part of the "crew"—he was going to get to work *with* Everette. Well, not directly, but he'd still be a tiny contributing part to putting on the show for the entire tour. Thirty-seven stops across the United States on the "Cut the Strings" tour. Maybe he'd even get groupies or get to party with Everett some night. Jesus, it was going to be awesome.

As he watched Everette about to disappear around the corner, the man he worshipped suddenly stopped and turned around. Chas panicked and quickly spun around himself to pretend to be moving a box; getting caught staring at the star of the tour as if he were in love was not a good way to start. Lifting up a black equipment box that was heavier than he expected, Chas almost dropped it when he heard the voice he had listened to for countless hours speak a few feet behind him.

"Aye, boy, who are you?" The fake indistinguishable European twang was unmistakable. Everette was speaking to *him*. Chas dropped the case, causing a loud slam, then quickly brushed his pants and spun around, pushing his hair back again, trying to be as smooth as possible.

"Uh, I'm Chas… I started today, I'm a roadie. Rex hired me," he said, lowering his voice an octave and adding in some gravel to his tone, hoping it made him sound older and more confident, even if inside his guts were twisting and squirming like they wanted out of his stomach. Everette looked him up and down and nodded. As he did this, Chas lost his breath. Everette was acknowledging him; he saw him, he knew his name, he came back to talk to him. Chas put one hand on his hip and with the other he tugged at his collar, hoping Everette was noticing his new suede jacket. He had to skip seven dinners to afford it after all.

"What is music to you?" Everette bluntly asked as if he were almost angry. Chas did not hesitate in his response.

"It is life." The second the words came out of his mouth, Chas saw the smile cross Everette's face.

"You are perfect… Have you met everyone here yet?" Everette asked, suddenly looking around the hallway; they were alone in the cavernous back hall of the amphitheater.

"No, just Rex really. I started, gee, like an hour ago. He told me to just be backstage here and that the guys will show me the ropes when they get in." Chas wanted to hit himself in the head for saying the word "gee" like some little kid, but he played it cool. Part of him wanted to rant about all the songs he loved and how he adored him, but Chas knew that Everette had heard that day in and out. He was also told not to talk to anyone in the band unless spoken to.

"Great. Come with me. I need some help in my dressing room. No one is here yet; the crew always sleeps in. I personally like coming in the morning to check out the stage alone. It's peaceful and lets me prepare in peace." Chas nodded up and down as if to say he totally understood, but inside he was screaming his head off like his sister did when the Beatles played on Ed Sullivan when they were kids. As they started to talk, Chas took a few deep breaths and finally got the confidence to speak up.

"I got into music because of you," Chas said,

looking forward as he walked next to his idol. He could feel the man looking at him, but he forced himself not to look.

"Really? Every roadie is a wannabe musician. What is your instrument?" Everette asked in a joking manner. Chas let out a small snort of a laugh.

"Guitar. I can't sing for shit, but I can shred. Nothing like you, of course, but I think I'm getting pretty damn good for my age." Chas was surprised he told him this, especially since he had never played in front of anyone, ever.

"I'd love to hear how you sound one day," Everette said coolly. Chas wanted to puke and run away at the same time, but he followed the man to the green door that had a gold star labeled "Everette" on it. Chas held his breathe as the door opened. The room was just like he had seen in movies and documentaries on rock stars. It had couches and cool lights and a table for food and, of course, a few guitars sitting around, though his eyes instantly went to the gold guitar case leaning against the wall. The simple word *Baby*, written out with crude pieces of black tape, was scrawled across the case. It was Everette's legendary gold Flying V electric guitar, the one that had traveled the world with him, that one he had recorded every song he ever wrote on.

"Jesus, is that really Baby over there?" Chas said before he could stop himself. He couldn't take his eyes off the box.

"Sure as hell is. If it wasn't for Baby, I wouldn't have a career," Everette said as he walked over and touched the box like it was a piece of art.

"Oh, I know the stories. Baby is your Excalibur," Chas whispered in a trance as he watched Everette snap open the case. Deep orange light streamed out of it, as if the gates of Heaven were opening. Everette reached a hand in, pulled out the stunning golden guitar, and closed the case, shutting off the battery-powered light. Chas swallowed hard as Everett held up the guitar and walked over to him, holding it out.

"I would let you play her, Chas, but you see, I have a problem. Baby has a broken string. And I need a new one." There was something different in Everette's voice; his accent was slipping and the tone became deeper. Chas looked at the guitar. He wanted to reach out and touch it, but he knew he shouldn't. Instead, he focused and looked at the broken strings. They were not metal like the ones he had always seen. These were a dark white with deep textures, unlike any strings he had ever seen. But, sure enough, one of them was missing.

"I could change it for you. Are there some extra ones in the case? Shit, I shouldn't do that. I was told to never touch the instruments," Chas said, suddenly broken from his trance of staring at the shining gold beauty in Everette's hand. His idol lowered the guitar a bit and took a seat on the table where the food would normally go before looking at his guitar with a smile of wonder and pleasure.

"Yeah, I'll go get someone and tell them you need a new string. I assume metal, right, but those didn't look... Rex said something about catgut strings in the interview, but I didn't think anyone uses those for electric guitars?" Chas said, looking around the room as if he might find some poster explaining strings. Everette looked up at him and shook his head.

"First of all, if you know Baby's name, you know I'm a vegetarian. I wouldn't use catgut; I'm not killing any animals for my music, it's sick. Second, the strings I use, you can't just get them anywhere. They are…handmade. Special. More powerful than any string you can buy." Chas started to feel a bit of panic and worry about the way Everette was explaining the strings, but he couldn't rationalize why.

"Um…ok, so…I'm confused. Do you want me to go get something? I'll do whatever you need. It is my job, really," Chas said, wanting to leave the room. The urge to get away from his idol did not seem natural, but something in his guts was telling him to run. Before Everette could answer, Chas turned and started to walk towards the door and spoke over his shoulder.

"I'll go see if I can find a payphone and call Rex at the hotel. I'm sure he will know what to do." Just as he was about to open the door, there was a loud strum on the guitar that was off key and, in a way, sounded like a dozen muffled screams. The sound made him stop in his tracks. He slowly turned around to see Everette, who was sitting on the table, one leg on the ground, with the guitar on his lap as if he were about to play a solo concert. The sound of the strings as Everette plucked them one by one was horrifying. Chas wanted to explode, to run away, to die rather than hear the awful noise any longer…yet he didn't move.

Everette stopped strumming. The sudden silence allowed Chas to breathe; he hadn't even realized he was holding his breath.

"*My* music. What does it mean to you?" Everette asked in a calm and serious tone. The comment made Chas relax and want to tell him the truth.

"Everything…" Chas let the word trail off before taking a big sigh and looking at his idol sitting there before him, holding the famed guitar.

"Your music makes me feel something. It makes me know I'm alive. It…it saved my life." Chas paused again, trying to read Everette's face to see if he sounded stupid or if his words were actually resonating with the man. At first, Everette had a stoic look of no emotion. It reminded Chas of the magazine cover he used to have taped to the wall next to his bed, the black and white one of Everette looking off into the distance. The only color on the cover was the stark words, *Rock Genius*. Chas started to realize this was all real, that he was with Everette and talking to him in his dressing room, when he saw the smile cross the man's face.

"How would you like to become part of my music?" Everette said, with a warm welcoming grin that almost seemed sly at the same time. Chas's mouth dropped open. Was the man asking him to play with him? He was too blown away to respond; he simply nodded his head up and down.

"That won't do, Chas. I need you to say out loud, yes, you want that." Chas smiled big, kept nodding, then forced the words out of his mouth.

"Yes, I want to be a part of your music, Everette," Chas said as he watched the man's grin grow wider before he licked, then bit his lip in concentration. Everette stood up, laid Baby down on the table, and then went over to the guitar case. Chas watched as the man opened it, the light spilling out again, then he reached inside and pulled out...a knife.

The site of the gold-handled knife, with its razor-sharp blade and serrated back side that looked like a hunting knife only a rock star could have, didn't worry Chas. It just confused him. Chas watched as Everette looked at the blade, smiled sadly, then walked towards him. It still didn't dawn on Chas to move or run or scream; it was Everette Freaking McDaniel walking towards him with a knife, not some nut job. This was a multi-millionaire with more Gold Records than he could hang up, a man who was so famous he couldn't go to a store or out to eat without security. A man like that wouldn't...

The knife went straight into his chest, fast and quick. It went in so easily, Chas actually had a momentary thought about how weird it was before the realization of being stabbed set in. Taking in a deep gasping breath, he could feel that the air in his lungs was no longer pressurized. He couldn't take a deep breath and his heart was vibrating and sputtering, not able to beat, as the blade was nestled deep inside of its chambers. The weird and confusing sensations, along with the fact that he was staring into his idol's face, was overwhelming. He thought he heard Baby's strings screaming in the background.

A second later, Everette's hand was on the back of Chas's head, guiding him to the floor. Breathing was getting harder, thoughts cloudier. Chas wanted to speak, wanted to ask questions, but he didn't know what to ask or if he was even capable of making words, even if his mouth was opening and closing like a big mouth bass gasping for air. As his vision started to blur, he heard a loud sucking noise, followed by release in his chest as the knife was pulled out. It wasn't until then that he started to feel the blood flow over him.

"When I was finding myself musically, I experimented with all sorts of things. I found that catgut strings on my electric guitar made for a rich and hardcore sound that was different than every other artist out there. It was my own sound. However, when I realized what they were made of… I was disgusted. Killing sheep and horses and other animals to use their intestines…the thought that my fingers where constantly rubbing up against their innocent insides…it horrified me." Chas caught a glimpse of Everette looking at the knife before it came down and started to slice open his stomach. There was no more pain, just the pressure of the sawing motion, then the foreign, tickly feeling of a hand moving around inside of him.

"Human intestines, on the other hand, I have no problem with. Our species is not innocent." Chas could hardly hold onto thoughts or see anymore. When he opened his eyes, he could see Everette dangling something long, ropy, and wet up in the air. It made him smile as he realized what was happening. Looking at Everett, he saw his idol smile back.

"That's right, Chas. If it wasn't for my strings, I wouldn't have my fame. I wouldn't be the god I am to you and so many others. And now, now *you*, will be a part of my legacy. Every cord I play, every riff I jam, every note I record, it will be you and your soul on full display for everyone," Everette said with such passion that Chas felt tears finally well up in his eyes. With the tiny bit of life he had left in him, Chas lifted his hand, formed his fingers into horns, and whispered, "Rock on."

The Vestige

It had been over two years since Madge had enough time to take a bath. Sure, she'd had quick hot showers, but they were always that: quick. And typically, they ended up with her opening the curtain and being startled by one of the triplets sitting on the carpet staring at her with spite in their eyes for leaving them alone for a mere few moments to clean herself. How they got out of the crib or play area was beyond her, but they always did, and they always found her. There was no such thing as alone time or privacy. The lack of being alone and the constant demands were eating away at her like some sort of slow-moving infection that would devour her insides for years until there was nothing left but a dried up and discarded shell. She was a "mom" though, so she forced herself to smile for her kids and lie to her family with a grin as she made comments like, "Everything is wonderful! They are God's little gifts! I couldn't imagine life without them!" Yes, she loved them, she guessed, but she also knew she would sell their souls to have a hot long bath.

After having what she called an "oopsie" moment, where she ran out of the house screaming that the children were trying to kill her, Bill, her near-invisible husband, promised to give her a night off to relax. Friends were a thing of the past and getting herself dressed and ready to go out on the town, alone, was not something she could mentally handle, but a bath…a bath she absolutely would adore. Of course, Bill would probably think he was heroic for watching his own children for two hours and want sex as a reward after the triplets went down. The thought of Bill on top of her, the very act that brought these monsters into her life, repulsed her, but she could lay there for five minutes in exchange for an hour in a bath. Madge just hoped she wouldn't reach up and choke her husband to death during his first thrust. The bastard got to go to work for nine hours a day, and on top of that, went out three nights a week, leaving her completely alone with no help and three demons destroying the house and her, but that was a thought for another time. It was time for a bath.

The large jacuzzi tub in their bathroom was the deciding factor in buying the house. The bathroom was a paradise: all tile, no windows, huge tub, a shower, and double vanity. It was gorgeous, but it was the tub that enthralled her. Madge had loved baths her whole life; the warm water and bubbles along with a few candles and music were her happy place. When she saw the large tub that she could disappear into, she turned to her dickhead husband—she didn't call him that back then—grabbed his hand, and said she wanted the house. The night they moved in they made love in the tub, and for the next three years she took a weekly bath, sometimes more. Even when she was pregnant, she would lay back in the warm, scented water, rub her stomach that protruded from the water, and think about how wonderful being a mother was going to be. Now the tub was filled with dirty laundry because the hampers were always overfilled by mid-week; the open space became the secondary place for soiled clothing.

After cleaning out the dirty onesies, the puke-stained blankets, and the random toys that were mixed in, Madge turned on the tap water and felt something unusual: a smile. She was actually smiling. As the water, boiling hot, screamed out of the faucet, she poured in her lavender oil soap and started to hum, something she forgot she used to do all the time when she was content. Turning around, she caught a glimpse of herself in the mirror; the humming stopped and the smile evaporated. The woman she saw looking back at her was unrecognizable. She was pale, her complexion flecked with blotchy red spots, her hair dry and frazzled. She wore a stained shirt she hadn't removed in three days and the bags under her eyes looked like luggage for an overseas trip. This is why Madge had avoided mirrors at all costs, because it was too depressing. Not that she was ever stunning, but she was presentable, clean, and happy looking once. Now she was a mere vestige of who she was.

Staring at herself in the mirror, she watched her red and puffy eyes as a few streams of tears came out and ran down her face before landing next to a stain on her shirt that could be puke, food, or something else. The dark thoughts started to seep in—the ones that she could never tell anyone. *They are my children. I love them. They are not trying to kill me,* she repeated over and over in her head to push out the intruding notions. Pushing them out was nothing but a momentary reprieve, as they were always lurking in the background like a stalker from the shadows. But today she was not going to let them win. She had a bath waiting for her. Madge stripped out of her clothing, threw it on the pile of laundry next to the tub, and then lit some candles.

Checking the water, she realized it was way too hot, then stepped in and plopped herself down so fast it sloshed the bubbles over the sides. The water burned every inch of her skin so intensely she wanted to scream, but she held it in as she sunk deeper, welcoming the pain. Pushing the auto start button on the jets, she shut off the water, grabbed a cloth, lay back, and covered her eyes as the tub came to life with a turbulent dance that was made to soothe.

***

Ten minutes later, the jets automatically shut off, leaving the room suddenly silent and still, bolting her awake from her half-asleep, half-dazed state. The lights in the room were off. She didn't recall doing that, but it made sense being that she lit candles. The sudden calming of the water and the flickering of the flames was a type of nirvana she knew she would have to fight Bill to have more of. If she could at least have a bath to look forward to every week, maybe she'd have something to hold onto. Sliding down so her mouth was under the water, her nose just slightly above it, she closed her eyes and thought of her favorite fantasy: her life before the children and the long list of things she was always going to do. Just as she thought about the bakery she always wanted to open, an all-too-familiar small hand grabbed a fistful of hair on her head and pushed her under the water. Madge sucked in a gasp of air to scream, taking in a full glug of soapy liquid into her lungs.

Panic set in just as she struggled, sloshing water over the edges and dousing all the candles. As she fought to get up for air, another hand grabbed her head and pushed her down further, then two more little hands grabbed her ankles and stopped her from kicking. They felt exactly like her little monsters' hands, but they were stronger—much, much stronger. She couldn't move. With her face underwater, her body convulsing and gagging from the lavender liquid already in her lungs, a twenty-pound weight slammed into her stomach. Madge knew it was one of her children jumping off the tub edge and onto her torso to help the others hold her down, even though the other two were already doing a hell of a job.

Kicking or knocking them off would certainly hurt them—something she was programed not to do as a mother, even if she thought of it daily—but air at this point was much more important. Pushing with her toes at the edge of the tub, she found she could slide her back a bit with the help of the flower-scented oils. Bending her knees slightly, she thrust up with all her might and slid out of their vile little grips and straight out of the water. The air she sucked in was sweet and welcome, but it was not enough, as the coughing and gagging that followed made her body have to fight to get the oxygen she needed. With her throat raw and her lungs finally satisfied, but burning, she blinked rapidly and looked for the demons that held her. She was alone. Leaning over the tub she looked for the little bastards; there was nothing. But in the soft glow of the nightlight, she saw a long path of wet…adult-sized footprints that led straight into the wall on the opposite side of the room from the door.

Madge stood up; naked and cold, she started to tremble as she reached for a towel and wrapped it around her aching body. There was no one. The door was shut. She would have been one-hundred percent positive that she could have fallen asleep, had a nightmare, and sucked in water, but there were *footprints*. The room was dark, but even in the blue hue of the nightlight, she could tell they were real prints right across the bathmat, then the tile, and into the wall. One print was even cut in half as if the wall didn't exist and someone had stepped right through it…

Flipping the light switch, nothing happened. The room stayed eerily soft blue, leaving pockets of darkness by the shower and toilet on the far end of the room. The breaker had popped a few times in the past when water splashed out, but why would the nightlight still work? Carefully and slowly, Madge stepped onto the carpet. Looking down, she saw her foot next to the wet print; it was almost twice the size of her foot, bigger than even Bill's would have been. Breathing was getting hard again. She'd lost her mind before the first year of raising the children was over, but this…this was an entirely different level of insanity. Or was it?

***

When they first moved in, they always joked about the house being haunted. They found handprints on windows they swore were not there the night before. Things disappeared often but they each blamed the other. Madge herself heard a voice clear as day several times, an audible male voice, but brushed it off as her mind playing tricks on her. Then Bill started to wake up in the middle of the night screaming that someone was in the room. Night after night, he would wail and freak out until she turned on the light and showed him no one was there. The doctor told him it was stress and gave him sleeping pills, which made Madge's life harder when the kids were born. Not only was she alone during the day, but she also had no help through the night with diaper changes and crying fits as nothing would wake the damn sloth he was. There was always something not normal that happened in the house, but nothing that warranted further research, let alone a passing thought, until the three homewreckers arrived.

Within a day of bringing the "children" home from the NICU, Madge thought something was wrong. One was always awake, always crying, and not from hunger or a wet diaper. It was as if something was torturing them and not letting them sleep. At one point, the crying never stopped. Unable to take it, Madge timed how long it went on for: three days, six hours, and twenty-three minutes of non-stop wailing, with each of the things that came out of her taking a turn, one by one screaming bloody murder. They only stopped when they left the house for a doctor's visit, where she was told nothing was wrong with them. As soon as they got home again, they started to cry.

Then the little bruises started to show up; small purple and green dots on their legs, arms, and stomach that they explained away as the children pinching each other in the cribs they shared. Madge thought it was more, like a rat or something was getting in with them, but Bill told her that was crazy and to just let it go. So, she did. Even when the kids started to do creepy things like babble to empty spots of the room or reach out to invisible arms, she told herself that babies do weird things—she'd never raised one, after all—and to let it go. The day she walked in on Spawn One gnawing on Spawn Two's leg, she yelled at them and looked up stories about children teething to tell herself it was normal. When Spawn Three jabbed a sensory block into Spawn One's eyes, as if he were trying to make it fit, causing an emergency room visit and an eyepatch for a month that never stayed on for more than a second, she again was told that babies do stupid things.

When they started to be mobile, hell broke loose. They bit everything, stuck things in every place that shouldn't have things stuck into, puked on every item, ripped apart what they could, and ruined every aspect of interior design she spent years creating. It was like they were a group of Gremlins, laughing every time they took yet another part of Mommy's home from her. Before long, they figured out how to bypass the baby gates and get out of their cribs. That is when Madge truly broke. Waking up to a child suffocating her by lying across her face or finding another spawn watching from the shadows of her room after she'd put them down an hour before in a locked room was soul crushing.

The day after the last one learned to walk, she found them all in the kitchen at three in the morning holding knives from the block on the counter that was impossible for them to reach. They were standing in a circle and talking their own babbling speech as if arguing about which one of them would get to cut Mommy first. When she flicked on the light and saw the shiny steak knives grasped tightly in their hands, her stomach dropped. When they all stopped speaking, then turned and looked at her with beady eyes and grotesque smiles of excitement, she screamed. Bill rushed down and...scolded *her* before racing by to take the knives away. Bill got a small cut on his left index finger; she was happy about that, but wished it had been more. After putting them all to bed, he screamed at her more and said she must have been "too tired" or "too dumb" to lock the gates and she must have left the knives on the counter or in the dishwasher (even though she told him that she only hand-washed knives). She knew the truth: they wanted to kill her. It was the night she stopped calling them her children or even thinking of them in that way. They were monsters.

The endless list of peculiar incidents that was tucked away in the back of her mind suddenly exploded forth, each torturous memory fighting for attention, all of them screaming, "I told you so" as she tried the light switch again. Nothing. Just as she wished for more light, two candles, which were still wet and soapy, sparked, flickered, then lit bright, six inch flames. Madge's insides turned to liquid. She felt exposed and terrified, but a slight wave of relief started to creep into her. *Let this be the end; just take me, destroy me, end this damn misery,* she thought to herself as she looked towards the wall waiting for something to come back out of it where the footprint disappeared.

Then five sharp fingers burrowed into her shoulder, making her scream and throw herself forward, causing the phantom talons to rip long, painful gashes. Madge might have wanted to die, but she didn't want pain. Throwing herself against the wall, she spun around, slid down, and sat right on the wet ghostly footprint. With the cold tiled wall against her bare back, she felt a bit more secure and ready to take on whatever was about to kill her, but there was nothing in the room. Trying to catch her breath, she felt the warm trickle of blood run down her shoulder just as the door handle started to shake violently. *She didn't lock the door,* Madge thought in a panic, but then quickly realized that it wasn't an intruder she had to be worried about. The thing was already in the room with her.

The last two candles lit and followed suit of the others with deep orange flames burning hot and high as if they were mini gas-powered flame throwers. It was as if whatever was in the room was preparing the scene for the grand finale of her life. The door handle continued to shake as the room filled with some sort of rumbling noise. Madge sat patiently watching and waiting, wanting it all to be over quickly. Even though she was ready, it was impossible not to be scared. When a dark mass appeared in the mirror above the sink the second before it shattered, she screamed and closed her eyes. A strong breeze started to tease her hair and cool her skin as it circled around the room like a serpent seducing its prey. The temperature dropped impossibly low.

Pulling her knees up to her chest, hard and scratchy hands that felt like they were made of jagged ice grabbed her ankles and then pushed down on them as if someone was leaning towards her. Squeezing her eyes tighter, she knew something was inches from her face; she could feel the presence of it, the iciness radiating off of whatever it was.

"Just do it," Madge whispered to the thing, begging it to hurry up and take her. The coldness came closer to her face as if she were about to be kissed by an ice sculpture...then she heard the door swing open, followed by a babbling "Ma, Ma." She instantly knew it was Spawn One, but she kept her eyes closed. Whatever was holding her down was probably doing it for her demon child so they could take the final blow, but a second after her own spawn spoke, the thing that was on top of her screeched and vanished. Opening her eyes, she feared seeing the child monster with a knife in its hand, but instead, she saw him smiling and looking at her with what looked like…love. For once, he looked like an innocent and cute toddler.

As the child stepped towards her, the candles suddenly went out and the lights in the room snapped on. It was like a cut in a movie, from a scene of pure horror to a normal bathroom with a smiling child looking at his injured mother.

"Ma, Ma, ok?" the child said, pointing to the wound on her neck. She recoiled a bit, but then realized the child seemed to know that the evil presence was gone; it was as if he were telling her it was alright.

"The…bad thing, it's gone? Did…did you make him leave?" The child put his hands on her knees, pushing them down so he could plop on her lap.

"No, gone. He here." Hearing this, all the blood drained out of Madge's face. Grabbing the monster on her lap, she was about to scream and push him away, but the sight of the other evil spawns walking into the room, each holding a steak knife tightly in their tiny little hands, stopped her cold. Letting go of the child, she once again decided to give up and just let this all end.

With a deep sigh, Madge watched as the door shut, the candles lit, and the dark shadow grew up out of the floor behind the things that were supposed to be her children…*her children*. They were supposed to be the loves of her life, that were supposed to make her complete and whole, not this vestige of a human ready to die on the floor because it was all just too damned hard. She was supposed to be willing to die *for them*, not *because* of them.

"Ready, Mama?" Madge heard Spawn Two say. She closed her eyes and nodded.

The Greater Good

At some point, someone has either asked you, or you heard some version of the theoretical questions, *if you were able to kill a baby Hitler, would you do it?* In the version you heard, it might have been a baby Hitler, a child, or even a teen version—basically, pre-homicidal maniac Hitler. How you went back in time is usually not part of the question; it's a moral question that I used to find very complex and interesting. If you knew you could stop the death of millions by killing a child or infant, would you do it? There are a lot of layers to this idea. First of all, if you were to change history like that, the entire world would be different; millions of more people would have lived and multiplied, numerous actors would not have Oscars for their performances in war movies, and every aspect of our entire being would cease to exist. Therefore, in my mind, in that instance, I would *not* kill a young Hitler. However, I propose to you the same question, but slightly different. If you knew, without a shred of doubt, that killing a child right *now* would save many lives, would you do it?

Murder is atrocious; very few people can kill. And even then, it's usually under great circumstances of misery, jealousy, rage or necessity. Very few people, usually sociopaths, can actually kill outside of those emotional peaks. Murdering someone when you are calm and collected is the definition of a sociopath. And even most of the ones who fall into that category wouldn't kill a child. Could you? Most of you would say no, no way. But I need you to really think about this: what if you knew, without a doubt, that a child standing in front of you would become a rapist, a murderer, or someone who would cause catastrophic damage to our society or world? What if you could save the life of so many by simply cutting off the air supply of a little infant in a crib or pushing a ten-year-old in front of a car? Would you do it? I never thought I could, but then I was shown the horrors I could prevent by doing something so simple yet so horrific and I realized it was worth every bit of my own personal pain and turmoil.

***

I've always had a deep belief in a higher power, but to say I was a religious man in a traditional context would be a stretch. I broke pretty much every one of the Ten Commandments, I never went to church, and I cursed God's name on a daily basis, which is why, when I was chosen for this mission, I was flabbergasted. Don't get me wrong, it's not a religious crusade and the ones who talked to me have never even alluded to me that they were angels or worked for God, but I knew in my bones that they did, because no one would know the things they do or have the power they have. Even the way they first showed up was, well, the only way to explain it is *magical*.

On Sundays, I liked to go out for a walk, jog, or

bike ride in Jackson Park. Well, maybe not liked, but I always tried to push myself to get at least a tiny bit of exercise each week and Sunday was just that day. That particular day, around nine, I was jogging around the lake…if you could really call my slow pace a jog. But hell, for being forty-three and slightly obese, it wasn't bad. Anyway, I was jogging and all of a sudden, a man in a green tracksuit, which in itself was so tacky it was odd, ran right into me. I even tried to move to avoid him, but every evasive move I made he kept right at me. Sure enough, he slammed into me like a linebacker trying to kill a quarterback, and knocked me down. Helping me up, he was apologetic. I was pissed, but I kept my calm and brushed off my shorts and tried to move on when the man grabbed my arm and told me to sit down on the bench with him to rest for a second. For some reason, though it was against my normal instincts, I sat next to him and looked the man in the face. He reminded me of someone, but I couldn't put my finger on it—maybe an uglier version of some young movie star that I just couldn't place? As I thought about who he could look like, he said my name, loud, clear, and unmistakable…*Johnathan.*

Before I could ask how he knew my name, he held a finger to his lips and nodded his head in the direction of the lake where a few small rowboats were floating around, a few people fishing, others lounging, and a few others trying to pretend they were on a crew team. I didn't understand what he was pointing at and looked back to him. He didn't say anything, but in my head, I swore I heard "*look harder,*" so I did. Then I noticed a small green boat with a boy and his father inside; the kid was probably twelve. He was trying to fish, his father guiding him carefully. Before I could even ask if it was them I was supposed to be looking at, the man nodded, then put a hand on my knee. What happened the second he touched it, I…I don't even want to explain, but I must in order for you to understand, at least a little. What I saw were a lot of young kids dead— students and young teens—and by the way it looked, I could tell it was a high school hallway I was seeing. The walls were covered in blood splatter. There were bodies everywhere, all of them shot. To me, the vision went on for what seemed like a solid five minutes; I felt like I was in the halls with the kids crying and hiding. I saw the bodies. I smelled the gunpowder and the sharp metallic scent of all the blood. My heart was pounding. Then I saw the shooter; he rounded the corner in slow motion, covered in all black, weapons dripping off his body. He held an assault rifle and pointed it right at me. I was never more certain of anything in my life than the fact that I knew in that moment it was the kid from the boat. Just as he was about to shoot me, poof, I was back on the bench, staring at the man in the green tracksuit.

The man stood up, looked at me with a very sympathetic frown, like a father who was telling his son he had to put down his dog, then walked away. It took a few seconds before I realized he didn't really say a single word other than my name, yet I understood without a doubt what he wanted me to do. I was in such shock that

I couldn't even muster words to ask questions, though I didn't need to. I knew I was chosen. I knew that man in the tracksuit was not a man, but an angel or some sort of higher being. I knew it was my job to stop this child from killing. I sat for an hour, watching the father and son fish. As they rowed to the shore, I walked around the lake and watched them. When they packed up their gear into their car, I sprinted to the other parking lot half a mile away where I was parked, jumped in my car, and raced over to their lot just in time to see them pull out. I then followed them for twenty minutes until they pulled into a modest home two towns over from where I lived.

I almost jumped up that second and ran over to the child and killed him on the spot, but part of me knew I had to get away with it, that I was now part of something bigger. How I knew this and all the other things along the way, I can't explain, but it was almost like a roadmap of information was given to me in that single touch. After writing down the address, I went home, showered, kissed my wife and kids, and had a normal "family" day with them all while I planned on how to kill a twelve-year-old. The next morning, I called out of work and went to the kid's house, parked down the street, and watched until I saw him walk out and head down the street to his bus stop. Looking around, I was thrilled to see him turn down a side street that had a length of woods and no houses for about forty yards. That was where I was going to have to do it.

While the kid in my vision was years older, meaning I had plenty of time, for my sanity, I had to do it that day. As the kid waited at the bus stop, which was just another forty yards from the wooded area, I raced off and went to a hardware store. In the parking lot, I sat and thought and planned. The child was still innocent; his death will be a tragedy and no one will ever know what he would have become and done, so I had to show some respect for who the child was at this moment in time. I thought of what I would feel if I lost my children and I cried for some time. I had to do as little damage as possible to the kid so his parents could have a nice funeral. With that, I chose strangulation. That way there would be no blood and less evidence.

Gloves, twelve-gauge metal wire, a landscaper's hat, sunglasses, and a large coat were the things I bought at the hardware store with cash. I then ate an early fast-food lunch, parked my car about a mile away from the bus stop area, and took a casual walk to the woods, where I looked around and then hid, knowing full well that I still had three or more hours until the child came off the bus. I spent those three hours praying; it was hard, as I hardly recalled any prayers, but I did the best I could. Then, at 3:05, I saw the child walking down the street, thankfully, on the side I was on. I crept as close as I could to the edge where I felt certain I was hidden, then waited for the boy to walk past. As soon as he did, I ran up behind him, slipped the wire around his neck, and pulled him back into the woods. It was so easy, it scared me.

I'll leave out the gory details of his death; besides, you know most of them from the news reports. What you don't know is that I saw his soul leave his body and it was beautiful. It was like in the movies; a glowing bright light in the shape of his body rose out of him, looked at me, and smiled before shooting straight up to the heavens. As horrible as the killing was, I knew the boy understood and was thankful that I had stopped him from doing the things he would one day do, because now he was going to Heaven rather than Hell for eternity.

Seeing his soul disappear into the sky was the greatest thing I ever saw, period. It filled me with such pleasure and joy that I sobbed and sobbed so long I forgot I was kneeling over the body of a child. When I looked down and saw his bloated little face, I truly understood how a body was merely a vessel. I got up, snuck out of the woods, got in my car, and left. As you know, they found him the next day, but no leads and no evidence. God was keeping me safe. That night as I fell asleep, I saw the number twenty-three in my head and I knew that was how many lives I had saved that day. I had the best sleep of my life that night.

***

While this opening statement is getting long, I felt the need for you all to understand how this began and to truly comprehend that while what I did was horrific from the outside, it was truly heroic and wonderful. The thirty-six children I have killed over the last nine years have saved exactly one thousand, four hundred, and twenty-one lives. The angels told me this. While to you guys I am a monster, to the heavens I am a warrior and hero. I have saved your children, your parents and lovers, your friends and your future leaders. The people I have saved will shape this world and save even more lives.

I can see that five of you on the jury have a cross around your neck and one of you has a cross tattooed on your finger. That means you believe in God and the Bible. If you truly do, then you know the stories in the Bible that are like mine. Abraham was told to kill his son and then there is the story of Eliseus on the way to Bethel. Children made fun of Eliseus for being bald, so God sent two bears to kill forty-two children. *Forty-two children*, mauled to death by bears, because God wanted them dead. It's in the good book; you can look it up in the Bible sitting right there by the stand, the one I'll have placed my hand on when I take the stand. Just flip to Kings, 2:23-34. God himself killed forty-two children, more than I did, simply because they made fun of a man for being bald. Until I was arrested, I was God's bear, only this time it was not out of vengeance; it was out of salvation. Most of you pray to Him every day, so why is it so hard to believe that He is still doing His work today? I will remind you of those stories through the trial and ask you, if you believe in God, then you have to believe He is still active today.

This trial will be long and hard and the prosecution will make me out to be the worst monster in history. They will question my sanity, but all I am asking you to do is think about your faith. You believe in a bible filled with fantastical stories. Why is it so crazy to think that God is *still* here and *still* doing His work through people like me? Lastly, I'd like you to think of the greater good. Could you kill one to save many? I can and I did, and I'm damn proud of what I have done and I will do my best to show that my actions were just and good. Thank you.

Omni-Vision

Delivering the evening paper was torture to Justin, even if it was only thirty houses on two streets. Every night he had to roll the papers and cram them into those cheap orange plastic bags, load them in his canvas sack, and then walk to each house with the strap cutting into his shoulder. He tried to use his bike at first, but he could never balance enough, so walking it was. Every step over the course of the hour it took him, which was right before he had to cook dinner, he thought of the Panasonic OmniVision VCR, *with remote*. All his friends were obsessed with Nintendo, but Justin loved his television. A game might have red and green eight-bit brothers who challenged your skills, but there were no funny situations with perfect families that you could pretend to be a part of. Like the Seaver family. *Growing Pains* might have been a new show, but man, they were an ideal family. Mike was so damn cool and the dad could solve anything. Justin just knew the mom would cook whatever he wanted and give him plenty of hugs. The last hug Justin had was two years ago before Mom died. If he just had a VCR, he could watch *Growing Pains* over and over and truly feel like he was a part of *their* family.

When his route was done, the bag hung in the garage right next to his black cherry BMX bike that his dad "found" in the trash one day, Justin would always head inside to wash the black ink off his hands, which never seemed to fully fade, as the next day another coat would be added to his pudgy fingers. Being a little after five, it was time for him to make dinner for Lou, his older brother, and himself. Dinner was supposed to be Lou's job, but after being threatened with a steak knife one night (which resulted in a four-inch-long scar along his left thigh), Justin promised to make dinner every night his father was working and to *never* tell that he had made dinner, *ever*. If Mike Seaver was his older brother, they might have a few fights, but they would end in family talk and hugs, not a scar. Most of the nights it was TV dinners, mac and cheese, hot dogs, and other easy-to-make things, but lately Justin had been branching out to cooking real food. Tonight, he was actually going to try and make a paprika chicken recipe he found in Dad's *Reader's Digest*—the issue with that long article about the Titanic that his dad made both of them read. Justin couldn't care less about the boat, but he fell in love with the recipe. It was a special night, after all: the season finale of *Growing Pains* was on and Justin couldn't wait. A fancy dinner beforehand would make for a perfect evening.

At eleven years old, Justin felt he was already a man, slapping on an apron, using knives and a gas stove—that was something only adults did, after all. The raw chicken was slimy and felt funny to Justin; before he put them in the pan, he squeezed the tenderloins through his fists and let it shoot out like the water-snake toy he loved playing with as a kid. Tossing them in the pan, he couldn't believe the sizzling and popping like mini grease fireworks. As he watched it cook, he licked the chicken goo off his fingers. It didn't taste too good, but the garlic salt and paprika that mixed in with the slime made him keep licking. When the chicken was done (which he could only tell by cutting them all in half), Justin was proud of himself. He had sautéed chicken and it looked pretty good! Placing the bright orange strips next to a plop of sticky chicken-flavored Rice-a-Roni on the plate, he felt a wave of pride he had never felt. *It was going to be a good night.*

Grabbing a New Coke out of the fridge, Justin picked up the plate, took a deep breath, and walked down the hallway to Lou's room. The door had a poster of Iron Maiden sloppily taped to it, the picture of the skeleton/robot/muscle-monster-thing (or whatever the hell it was) always scared the shit out of him; he never looked at it and he even had to move his bed to a different spot in his room so he wouldn't see it when he looked out of his door at night. With his hands full, he lightly kicked the door twice and yelled out, "Dinner is ready, Lou. Made something new." For a split second he giggled at the rhyme, but then the door opened so fast it made him jump. Justin had a habit of not looking at Lou, just like he didn't look at that monster on the poster. Holding out the plate, he stared at it over daring looking at his brother's zit-covered face and spikey, jet-black hair. Sometimes he wondered if Lou was so mean because his entire face was made up of a million little red mountains filled with pus.

"Where the fuck is the barbecue sauce?" Lou barked as he yanked back the plate and Coke at the same time.

"Oh, it has a lot of seasoning, you shouldn't need any on…" Justin knew better than to talk back, but he was so excited about the meal, he simply forgot. The foot hit his stomach flat, the toe of the shoe right over his belly button and the heel right above his crotch. It wasn't so much the impact as the thrust behind it that was the worst. It sent him flying, completely leaving the ground. Justin landed on his ass first; his back slammed the ground next, and then his head in one fast succession that sent bursts of pain through his body. Crying was quick and easy for him, but this time it came instantly. Lou marched down the hall in his massive black boots, and stepped squarely on Justin's chest. At the same time his chest was crushed, Lou said, "I'll fucking get it, you pussy." The two quick pops happened in concert with pus and sy, like tiny twigs snapping, one after the other, to the word. Justin felt them inside his chest, but also eerily heard the noise in his ears, as if his brain was telling him, *oh shit, you hear that?*

As he heard the fridge door open, he took the opportunity to roll on his side, pushing the front of his body against the wall for protection. As his cheek stuck to the yellow linoleum floor, he stared at the flower-print wallpaper, bracing for what might happen next. The pain was unlike anything he'd ever felt, but he knew if he hadn't moved, Lou would step on his chest again. Thankfully, this time as he passed, it was just a steel-toe-tipped kick to the ass. When the door slammed shut, Justin fell onto his back and sucked in a breath for the first time. It felt like Freddy Krueger had slammed his rusty blades right into his chest, then twisted. There was no question that his ribs were broken. Over the course of the next ten minutes, he cried and did his best to slow his breathing to stop Freddy from jabbing him over and over again. The pain did not get better, but he had to get up and find some of Dad's aspirin in the cabinet, fast.

Justin pictured himself as John Rambo getting ready for his final fight, for he would certainly have to fight against the pain and get up. And that is just what he did, but the tears never stopped falling and Fred never stopped jabbing. After taking four aspirin, Justin fell into the stool at the counter right in front of his plate and sobbed. The crying was making the pain worse. Staring at the beautiful meal he had just cooked next to the glass of soda losing its fizz and knowing there was no way he could eat it, Justin once again thought about the Seavers. They never had to eat alone; Mike would never hurt Ben like this. *Why couldn't I just have a family like that?* One where there were family dinners, where a dad would play basketball after eating and then watch television together. Putting his head down on the counter, he enjoyed the coolness against his skin, but he had to be careful not to get too close to the edge; that sucker was sharp and had hurt him before. Within a few seconds, Justin passed out.

***

"Come get my plate and bring me another Coke, fucktard!" The scream woke Justin from a dream of playing hoops with Mike and Dr. Seaver. For a beautiful split second, he forgot that there was a cold dinner he was unable to eat in front of him and that he had a few broken ribs, but the second he breathed, his reality filled his lungs. Lou yelled a second time, but Justin did not get up. He simply couldn't. The door slamming open and the stomping of the boots would normally scare him, but with an empty stomach and pain that was too hard to handle, Justin hoped Lou would just end all of this for him. As the steps got closer, he braced for just that to happen.

"What is wrong with you? Why didn't you eat? That shit was good; you need to make it more." This was rare for Lou, who was normally raging in any conversation unless Dad was in the room.

"Justin, fucking answer me."

Justin tried to sigh but winced and cried before whispering a reply.

"Ribs…you broke my ribs. Can't breathe…or talk. Hurts too much," he said in a wheezing whisper. Hearing Lou take in a massive breath as he set down his plate, Justin felt a pang of jealousy for how easily air filled his brother's lungs.

"You got to be kidding me?" Lou said, clearly annoyed. Suddenly he felt hands spin him around and two fingers start jabbing his ribs all over. The scream he let out was unlike anything that had ever come out of his mouth before.

"Shit," Lou said in his own whisper as he tried to keep Justin from falling off the stool. He wanted Lou to finish him, to just stab him with a knife like he'd threatened so many damn times and end all of this, but instead his brother backed away, pointed a finger at him, and yelled.

"You fucking let Dad know about this and you are dead. Seriously dead. A few ribs won't kill you. Clean up the kitchen, ice that shit, and keep your mouth shut." Lou then reached across him and took Justin's plate and soda and walked back to his room. *There was the Lou I knew.* It took him nine times longer than normal, but he cleaned the dishes and the counters then grabbed frozen peas and went into the living room to ice his ribs and watch television. It wasn't a second too early; it was only ten minutes before the season finale of *Growing Pains.* At least he could disappear into their happy lives for a few minutes. Just as that thought ran through his head, the doorbell rang.

Justin wanted to cry. He didn't want to move, but he knew if he didn't get the door by the second ring, Lou would throw a fit. Moving with extreme care, but fast as he could, pain shot off like black cat fireworks, rapid fire explosions all through his chest. In the kitchen, ten steps from the door, the bell rang again. Justin mumbled half a dozen swears and hurried his pace. Pulling aside the curtain, he saw a man in a brown frumpy suit and small matching hat holding a large briefcase. The guy was the epitome of a door-to-door salesman. He hadn't seen one of those since he was really little, when he used to be home with Mom and Lou was in school, back when things were okay. Justin just wanted him to leave, so he opened the door, preparing to tell him he was not interested, but the mustached man spoke first.

"Evening son, are your parents home? I have a deal they simply can't pass up!" The sun was just starting to set behind the man. *Why the hell was he coming out so late?* This thought briefly flashed in Justin's head, but then the pain spoke up and told him to get rid of the man fast so he could lie back down.

"We don't want any," Justin said as he started to push the door shut, but then the man said three magic letters that made the pain not so bad.

"A VCR? A kid like you could tape all his favorite shows. You'd never have to miss another and you could watch them over and over. Hell, you and your brother could watch one show while taping another, ain't that a thing?" Justin pulled the door open a bit wider, gave the guy a suspicious look—*how did he know I had a brother?*—but didn't respond. After an awkward moment, the man kept talking.

"I can have you set up in five min'. I'll even install it and give you a tutorial. You'll have it working before *Growing Pains* even starts! Best part, you alone can afford the payments; just give me your weekly pay from your paper route and in two months it is all yours." The voice was so soothing and convincing, Justin stepped back and the man walked right in. Justin eyed the suitcase wondering how a VCR could fit inside. It seemed impossible. There were also a lot of other questions swirling in his head, but things were getting cloudy and he just didn't care. *He was getting a VCR.*

Sitting in awe, Justin watched the man as he expertly weaved a wire behind the wooden frame of the television, plugged in the device and then sat it on top. As the orange and green screen lit up, Justin felt a smile, bigger than any he'd had since Mom died, cross his face. The man knelt down and pushed some buttons and within a few seconds the time was there. It was three minutes before *Growing Pains* was to start. *I need blank tapes,* Justin thought at the exact second the man pulled out a pack of three VHS tapes, tightly wrapped in cellophane, red and white writing and some logo he had never seen before blazed across the packaging. Using his finger as if it were a knife, the man sliced open the side, pulled out a tape, slipped it out of its sleeve, and slid it into the machine. The sound it made while entering, the clicking and churning noises, was so beautiful.

"Now son, listen here," the man said in a serious tone as he sat down on the coffee table—something his father would have been furious with. Justin looked at the clock, less than a minute to go, but just as he was about to speak up, the man put up a finger and kept talking.

"'*Pains* is taping; you can watch it and fast forward through the commercials. I need you to hear me first. There are some important rules to owning a VCR." The fear of missing a show was a fear deep inside of Justin's chest, but he sat and stared at the man, wondering how the VCR could record if the television was off.

"A VCR is controlling time. You can rewind time

to experience the best moments and even fast forward through the boring parts. It is power. Use it wisely, especially those tapes. Those are from my private collection; you can't get those in stores and you only get three with a purchase." With that, the man stood up, flipped his hat on in a gesture that seemed unnatural, and then winked at Justin.

"Just need a handshake, son. I don't do paperwork; a handshake seals the deal. I'll come to collect the first payment in one week's time. This is a golden opportunity. Don't mess it up." Without thinking, mostly wanting the man to just leave, Justin put out his hand. The man grabbed it, almost crushing his bones. Justin could feel a slight tingle of static electricity whirling around their hands as the man held his, pumping up and down a bit too long. When the man let go, there was a tiny static shock that hit the tip of all five fingers, all in a row, in quick succession, *zap, zap, zap, zap, zap.* As he stood there looking at his fingers, he heard the door gently shut.

Not even a few seconds later, the pain in his ribs returned with a fury, which took him by surprise as he had forgotten all about the broken bones the entire time the man was there. This caused a wave of confusion in his head; pain and anger mixed with the pure joy of having his own damn VCR. Holding the remote in his hand, he looked at it in awe. *It is all mine.* Doing his best to ignore the pain, he lay back down on the couch, grabbed the bag of peas that had fallen on the floor, placed them on his chest, and closed his eyes, the remote still held tightly in his hand. He could rest. The television schedule no longer needed to control him. *He* controlled television.

***

"What the hell is that?" Lou's scream woke Justin from a dead sleep. He jumped up, pain shooting through his body. Ignoring it, he stood up to get between Lou and the VCR, as Lou was known for destroying things Justin loved. Lou stood there in front of him, his face scrunched up in disgust and curiosity at the new machine. Justin steadied his breath—*Christ, my ribs hurt,* he thought—before trying to explain.

"I bought it with my paper route money. It's mine, but if you aren't a dick, you can use it, too. Just…just ask, please, ok? It's expensive." Hearing the words come out, Justin was proud of himself for, sort of, standing up to Lou. Unfortunately, Lou stopped looking at the machine and turned his gaze to the wet stain on Justin's shirt where the peas had melted. Instantly, Lou shot out his arm, his finger pointing hard, and jabbed it right into Lou's chest. Justin could feel the rib move inside of him as Lou pulled back and called him a donkey dick, one of Lou's favorite terms ever since seeing *Weird Science* the year before. As Justin crumpled into a ball and fell to the floor, he reflexively squeezed his hands shut, forgetting he still had the remote in his right hand. Just as his knees were about to hit the ratty old brown carpet, he froze in midair, in an impossible position.

Panicking, Justin worried he was having a stroke like his uncle did, or some sort of mental break causing him to hallucinate his virtual floating stance, but when he turned his neck, which was hard to do, it felt like he was fighting massive weights. He saw Lou frozen in mid-stride, one hand reached to the VCR. *A VCR is controlling time.* It was impossible… Fighting the stiffness of moving, he looked at the remote. Sure enough, his thumb was pushed down on the pause button. *No way.* With a bit of effort, he pushed his thumb down and he instantly fell to his knees, all the pain shooting through him. The pain was so intense, he instantly hit the pause button again, shutting off the hurt, all sound, and their movement.

Laughing out loud, he slowly moved each limb in his body until he was able to fight against whatever force that was keeping them frozen. It took some practice, but after what seemed like ten minutes, he was able to move freely. Feeling comfortable, he made his way over to Lou to examine him and see if he was conscious or completely frozen. Lou looked like some sort of wax figure, perfectly still and lifelike, his arms reaching out to the VCR. It was absolutely insane. Lou's eyes were wide open, yet when Justin moved his hands in front of them, there was not the slightest reaction. This made Justin laugh more. He had not gotten this close to Lou in years. Standing near his face, knowing Lou couldn't do anything to him…the punch was fast, but not that great. It would have been liberating, had Lou moved at all, but his face felt like a steel beam. Shaking his hand, Justin cursed then laughed to himself. His knuckles were going to be bruised, but it was worth it. Reaching out with one finger, he poked his brother's face. It was hard, as if his brother were a statue. Justin's jaw dropped in wonder.

After settling in with his new reality, Justin built up the courage to try the rewind button. Sure enough, that worked as well. As he lightly pushed it down, he felt an invisible force trying to pull him backwards to recreate all the steps and actions he had just done, but he was able to fight against them as he watched Lou walk backwards, then reenact the jab, only this time to empty air and then march in reverse right out of the living room. Once Lou was gone, he hit pause and thought for a moment. *How far can I rewind...? What if... Mom?* Looking down at his ribs, he wondered if he could go back far enough to stop them from being broken; that would be a start, but that was *before* the salesman came, so would it work? Could he fight against time and these forces to keep the VCR, or would the man simply pack it up? Wait, even if he did, the man would just bring it again. *Rewind.*

Staying seated on the couch, Justin watched the clock spin backwards and the sun outside start to rise again. He felt like a god. After a few moments, the salesman walked backwards into the room, but as soon as he was in front of Justin, the man stopped and turned towards him. The world kept moving around them as the man fought the forces as well.

"Son, be careful. Time is power." The man suddenly walked out of the room, pushing against the rewind, yet time kept going backwards. He was leaving the VCR there; he was letting Justin rewind further.

***

Paused in the moment after the moment his ribs were crushed, Justin felt free and calm. The world was silent and there was no fear of his brother slamming into the room to hurt him some more. Time was stopped. There was no wind, no noise at all; the earth was shut off. Lying still on the couch enjoying the silence, he thought about how he could sleep without the fear of being woken up. He could sleep for as long and as deep as he wanted. Being more tired than he was excited to play with this new power, he held tightly to the remote and slipped off into a dreamless sleep. When he awoke, everything was exactly the same and he had no clue how long he'd slept, but it didn't matter, did it? Getting up, he walked around the house, looked at the food on the counter that was consistently staying warm, and then looked at Lou. His brother was half inside of the fridge, looking for the damn barbecue sauce he'd forgotten. For some reason, Justin was scared to go back further than he did, but he also did not want to relive the moment his ribs broke. Looking at the food some more, he realized he wanted to eat the damn meal he'd cooked, and he hit rewind.

Within seconds, Lou had walked backwards to his room, the door shut, his ribs were no longer broken, and the other plate was back on the counter. Hitting play, he instantly jabbed at his ribs. They were better. *This is insane.* This time, Justin grabbed the barbecue sauce along with the plate and brought it down the hallway. Lou was still an asshole, but Justin did not end up on the floor; instead, his brother accepted the food and let him be. He couldn't help but smile and laugh while enjoying the ability to take deep breaths. Sitting down in front of his plate, he smiled, picked up his fork, and cut a big bite of chicken and greedily put it into his mouth. It was absolutely delicious. Looking at the remote, which he purposely set far back from his plate to make sure he got nothing on it, he smiled and thought about how life was going to be better. Taking his second bite, he heard Lou's door fly open. Justin nervously grabbed for the remote, but Lou was already there. His brother was upon him so fast it was almost as if the tape had skipped.

"That was fucking delicious. Give me your plate and make this more often, ass wipe." Just as Justin grabbed the remote, Lou came up from behind, hunched over Justin, and clamped down around both of his wrists. This was a move that Lou loved; he called it the "Puppet Master" because he could control Justin and make him do whatever the hell he wanted. Thankfully, Justin was able to hit pause, freezing time once again, but Lou's grip was too tight, and his brother was practically on top of him. He couldn't maneuver his way out of it as Lou was stone hard again. Justin had to push rewind, but his grip on the remote was so awkward that he had to adjust it to try and get his finger on the correct button. Of course, that is when he dropped the remote. It clanked on the counter, teetered on the edge, then fell off to the linoleum. In a loud crack, the battery compartment door shot off and two double A's spilled out. Justin was stuck.

Lou's body was solid, like a marble statue carved by some sick artist to be a torture device. The hands around his wrists were clamped so tight that his fingers were starting to fall asleep. No matter which way or how hard he pulled, he couldn't loosen the grip, not even in the slightest. When he pushed back against Lou, it was like trying to move a pillar. Over the next ten minutes (at least he thought it was that long; there was no time after all), Justin screamed and thrashed, he kicked, he pulled and yanked and moved every possible way. Lou did not budge an inch; his grip did not change. The only change was that the skin on Justin's wrists was starting to tear open a bit.

Settling into a slow sob, resting his head on the counter, Justin's mind started to race. *Was the rest of the world frozen? What happens if I die? Did I kill the world? Wait, how long will it take me to die? I'll starve to death; it will take days. Days of Lou keeping me locked in the puppet master position, his face and chest smashed up against my back and head. I won't even know how many days, let along hours, it will be, because nothing will change. I don't even know how long I've been sitting here. I can't do this, I can't, I can't.*

After sulking for a few more minutes, Justin tested how far he could move his head. If he slammed it back into Lou's face, then down on the sharp edge of the brown linoleum counter, he could kill himself. It could work. He could break his nose and cut his face enough that he'd bleed to death, and if the impact didn't kill him, it would at least knock him out long enough that he wouldn't have to live through the pain of the position he was in and the eventual starvation. All he wanted was to not feel the pain of his ribs anymore; now he was in more pain and contemplating his own death. *Fucking Lou.* The thought of dying was terrifying, but the pain in his wrists and the growing claustrophobia were stronger.

"Show me that smile again…" Justin sang through a sobbing cry, right as he slammed his head back into Lou's stone face. Lou's nose felt like a steel point and it did the same damage of one, instantly cutting a deep gash into Justin's scalp. The pain made the tears come harder, but he couldn't stop. Slamming his face forward on the edge of the counter—that damn sharp counter—did its job. Justin's nose snapped and popped just like his favorite cereal. The blood poured quickly as fireflies zipped in front of his vision. If he were standing, he would have fallen to the floor. Resting a second, the pain started to seep in; it was awful and he wanted it to stop, but there was only one way to stop it. *Slam back, slam forward, pause, orientate, slam back, slam forward, slam back, slam forward.*

As Justin faded in and out of consciousness, blood flowing freely from the lacerations on the back of his head and the cuts and slices on his face, he thought of the Seavers. The images were fractured and confusing, but they made him smile. Playing basketball with Mike, dinner with the family, Dr. Seaver giving him advice and so many damn hugs. It was wonderful; it was what a family was really like. When enough blood had finally drained out of him to put him into a deep sleep, Lou's hand suddenly let go, but Justin had no clue.

***

"What the mother fuck!"

Lou jumped back. There was blood everywhere—all over the counter, the floor, even on his face. But he had absolutely no clue what the fuck was happening. He had just grabbed Justin's hands like he always did. After several long seconds of panic, Lou grabbed Justin's shoulders and shook him, but his brother quickly slid off the chair sideways and landed on the floor with a sickening thud. *Was he dead?* Lou bent over and shook his brother some more. Justin's face looked like it had been chewed on by Cujo. Even the back of his head had massive cuts. *What happened? Did…did I do this? Holy shit, I have to fix this.*

Just as Lou rolled Justin over onto his back, there came a knock at the door that made him scream out loud. Looking over his shoulder, he could see a man's silhouette through the dingy curtain. "Go the fuck away!" Lou screamed in a panic, not knowing what else to do as he contemplated putting pressure on the wounds. *But which one?* The knocking came again. With pure rage, Lou jumped up, grabbed the handle, and swung the door open and screamed at the man to leave, using half a dozen swears in the process. When the man hardly reacted, Lou calmed himself down and stared at the guy in the hat, who was looking beyond him into the kitchen. Lou looked back himself, and that is when he saw the remote control on the floor. He hadn't noticed it before, and in fact, he had never seen that remote. Batteries were on the floor next to it, but the oddest part was the blood had encircled it, but without touching it, as if it were pushing the blood away. As he started to contemplate this, the man spoke.

"I guess he didn't know that all VCRs un-pause after a while so it doesn't cause stress on the tape." The man raised an eyebrow and laughed lightly. Lou looked at him with pure confusion and rage boiling up. Just as Lou kicked the door, he watched the man raise a hand and push a button on an identical remote. Lou planned on tackling him, but when he got through the door, the man was gone. He'd simply vanished. Like a maniac, Lou ran down the driveway looking for him, but there was nothing, not even a car pulling away. *I'm losing my mind.* Running back inside, he didn't notice the remote on the floor was gone, the clearing of blood starting to fill in.

An hour later, after forcing himself to call for an ambulance, Lou found himself handcuffed, sitting in a hospital bed, waiting to have his mental state examined. Just as the doctor walked in, *Growing Pains* started on the television hanging from the wall.

Eighteen Letters

Twenty-seven years and forty-nine days, Martha thought to herself as she walked into Linden, Gillette & Connor Accounting Services. *Nineteen years, three-hundred, and sixteen days down.* The constant counting of numbers and keeping track of her steps—one-hundred and forty-two from her car to her desk, thirty-six to the bathroom—had been exhausting when she was younger, but now it was second nature and just like breathing. Martha simply *had* to count. When someone spoke to her, she counted the number of letters in each of the sentences, then added them all up when they finished talking to give herself the total letters spoken during the conversation. Carl, two cubicles and four steps away, talked very little with an average of four hundred words of conversation a day. Connie, one cubical and one step away, talked the most with four to five thousand a day. Martha hated Connie; she made her count too much.

Martha was always the weird girl growing up, the overweight one who wore glasses and handmade sweaters, who talked very little but made every academic honor possible. All her teachers said she'd be something great one day because she was a "genius." Looking at her tiny cubicle with the torn gray fabric and three coffee stains on the right side, she counted the six letters in "genius" and sat down. It had been her cubicle since she was nineteen and took a temporary accounting job while in college. She'd never left the job and never moved out of the same drab cubicle. It had been her space for almost twenty years and would be for the next thirty as well, as long as the company was still around. Martha was fine with that. She liked accounting, her cubicle was comfortable, and she had a nice home with three cats and a girlfriend she saw twice a week for exactly four hours each time. Life was just the way she wanted…until they hired the man with too many letters in his name. *Twenty-seven, thirty-three,* including the suffix. Franklyn Wainwright Pennyworth Junior.

Franklyn had been hired as middle management when respectable-length, *eight letters,* Joy, no middle name, Smith, retired last month. The short balding man looked to be fifty, but made sure everyone knew he was only forty. He wore cheap wrinkled suits and was loud— so loud that Martha could hear him over the noise-canceling headphones she wore when crunching numbers (as hearing outside conversations messed up her real counting).

Franklyn's desk was twenty-six steps away, in the middle of an open area surrounded by cubicles to show his role was important. Martha had never once heard Joy when she was at her desk. She could hear every word Franklyn spoke, however. It drove her insane. Worse, the man talked so fast he made the Micro-Mini-Machines man sound like a turtle. Martha could count fast, but she'd never encountered someone who could talk so fast she had to struggle to keep up. It was exhausting.

At the end of Franklyn's first week, after talking to her therapist, she'd gathered enough courage to send an email to him about his volume control. Thirty-one seconds after she sent it, Franklyn was over her shoulder ranting at her about how his voice was "not loud" and that he didn't bother anyone. He spun around six times asking everyone in the office if the volume of his voice was too loud, using three-hundred and thirty-one words. There were zero words in response. No one spoke up. No one agreed with Martha. Her face burned; she had a hard time breathing. When he walked away, she faced her computer and cried for six full minutes, cursing every one of her co-workers. She had to stay there for thirty more years, yet she couldn't listen to Franklyn for another minute.

***

That night, sitting with her girlfriend Marissa, holding hands on the couch and watching an old Buster Keaton silent film (she was obsessed with silent films because they were the only thing she could watch and not have to count the words), she paused the movie and spoke. Normally they spoke very little during the four-hour slots. They held hands for two hours while they watched silent films. Afterwards, they would move into the bedroom, undress and silently hold each other for one hour, then move apart, and Marissa would then speak for thirty minutes while they lay in bed. The last thirty minutes were spent getting dressed and having a coffee in the kitchen while discussing plans for their next date. They would then kiss three times on the lips and Marissa would leave.

"I have to leave my job," Martha said breathlessly. Marissa, who looked very similar to Martha, only with blonde hair, not black, stared straight ahead and looked scared. Martha felt awful that she was breaking their routine; pausing the films was a no-no. She felt especially bad that it was for *her* problems, but she couldn't help it.

"The man is awful, just awful and no one else will say anything to him. I cannot do my work correctly and it's upsetting me very much. I think I might have to up my medications or...or find a new job." Martha hated speaking that many letters at once. It made her dizzy and the idea of getting another job almost made her throw up.

"No, Martha," Marissa said, but then didn't follow it up. Martha waited, finger hovering over the pause button, wondering if she should let Harold Lloyd move from his precarious situation on the edge of a roof. Just as she was about to push play, Marissa spoke again. "Stop him from talking. Now push play please, we are off schedule now." Without hesitation, Martha pushed play and Harold fell through the roof. They both giggled, but Marissa's words—*eighteen letters*—replayed over and over in her head. *Stop him from talking. Stop him from talking.*

***

Later, after the three kisses, Martha was alone and ready

to make plans. How could she stop the man from talking? Sitting on the edge of her bed, going through her nightly routine of putting lotion on her feet, the eyedrops on her night stand caught her attention. *Consuming eye drops can cause violent diarrhea.* Martha recalled this from the time she had spent over six hours and fourteen minutes on the toilet her junior year in high school when Brad—*such an ugly name; no wonder it's four letters*—played a "prank" on her. Franklyn always had coffee on his desk, and all the cubicles faced away from him. She could sneak up when he was on his morning break, which he always took at exactly 10:15 with three of the "guys" in the office. He joined them for a smoke even though he didn't smoke. She could put eyedrops in his coffee. The idea made her excited, but it also made her feel sick with fear and anxiety.

Martha only left her desk twice a day for bathroom breaks. She ate lunch at her desk. Breaking that routine would be hard. It would add extra steps to count and change her entire day's total number, but it would be worth it. She would have the rest of the day free of Franklyn's incessant talking. As she lay down to sleep, she put exactly two drops into each eye and made a mental note to stop at the store in the morning to get a fresh bottle.

***

After the store, Martha was already four-hundred steps over her normal total. It upset her, but she was letting the excitement of shutting up Franklyn win the battle of emotions. Waiting the few hours until break was torturous, but just like clockwork, Franklyn and the three other guys got up at 10:15 and went outside. Part of her was happy the other people followed schedules so regularly as well. She counted in her head to two hundred, to make sure they were down the elevator, before taking the cap off of the eyedrops and pulling out the small plug so it would pour easier. With a deep breath, she stood up, turned around, and walked the twenty-six steps to Franklyn's desk. Using a sheet of paper to hide the bottle, she pretended to set the paper on his desk as she poured the entire bottle into the ugly, green-stained mug that was still half full. She was then on her way to the bathroom to keep up the act of why she got up.

Two-minutes and forty-three seconds later, Martha was back at her desk. She was breathing hard, but a giddiness and excitement she had never felt was rushing through her veins like tiny rocket ships racing through her body. Instead of getting back to work, she watched the reflection of the door to the hallway on the corner of her computer monitor, waiting for it to open. When the doors opened at exactly—

Wait, how long has it been? Martha realized that she hadn't been counting that entire time. It sent her into a panic, but it also thrilled her. She could recall on one hand the times she'd stopped counting without trying. Letting out a laughing snort, she looked around and pointed to her screen to pretend she got a funny email.

Thankfully, Connie was out that day; otherwise, she would have asked what was so funny.

Over the next twenty minutes, she again pretended to work as she watched Franklyn sip his cold laced coffee. And again…she didn't count. When Franklyn got up and went to the breakroom for another cup, Martha was giddy like never before. It was going to kick in soon. He would be in the bathroom and out of her head for the rest of the day. She was so proud of herself for taking the matter into her own hands that she wanted to celebrate.

Everything happened so quick. Franklyn started to moan obnoxiously loud, stood up, spasmed as if he were having convulsions, made awful faces, then ran to the bathroom. Seconds later, a smell filled the entire office, making everyone gag—especially Martha, who hated foul smells. Jim, one of Franklyn's smoking buddies, walked over to their boss's desk, looked down, then whispered to everyone that there was shit on the floor. While grossed out, Martha felt a warm tingle of pleasure through her body. Everyone was laughing and looking at Franklyn, *not her*. Seconds later, moaning and swearing came from the bathroom in an endless diatribe. Franklyn was *not* embarrassed, not at all; instead, he was yelling for someone to come in there to help him. His other smoking buddy, the wiry Stan, went in like a brave soldier. Two minutes later, he came out with a long list of orders.

"Tiffany, take petty cash and go get some new clothing and some Imodium A-D for Franklyn. Jim, go to IT and get one of the loaner laptops for Franklyn to use in the bathroom. Martha, get some cleaning supplies from the closet and clean up the mess on the floor. The rest of you get back to work."

Martha stopped counting the letters when she heard her name. Her jaw dropped open at the same time. They wanted *her* to clean up the…mess? Granted, the janitor only came at night and there was no one they could call that would fit that duty, but, her? Franklyn was doing this to her on purpose. Did he know what she had done, or did he just really hate her that much? She sat frozen, unsure what to do. She'd never had to clean up anyone else's filth before. She couldn't handle it. She'd throw up. And worst of all, everyone would watch her on her hands and knees wiping up Franklyn's feces. There was no worse humiliation. But if she didn't do it, it would sit there until he came out and then he would be even angrier. His vengeance would last as long as he worked here. Martha couldn't breathe. It was all too overwhelming.

Dry-swallowing three Ativans, Martha stared at her screen. She had caused this situation; she had tried to stand up for herself and now things were ten times worse. *Clean it up or go home?* She asked herself over and over again in her head. The worst part was that no one had spoken up for her. No one had said it was wrong to make her clean it. They'd all just gone back to work. Someone had sprayed pumpkin spice air freshener, but other than that, they all ignored the situation. Worst of all, Martha could still hear Franklyn's loud mouth in the bathroom.

***

That night, Martha stared at her frozen dinner cooling on the table in front of her, too disgusted to take a bite. She had taken three showers to try and get the memory and revulsion off of her, but she still felt horrid. Cleaning the liquid puddles of thick brown and black goo while everyone in her office watched…it broke her in ways she knew she would never recover from. Not only would no one in that office ever respect her again, they would all know they could make her do anything. Martha was ashamed of herself, but more so, furious at Franklyn and his damn loud mouth.

Slowing her breath, Martha caught herself replaying the day's events and trying to count the words said in her memory. This was a bad habit she only did when things were getting out of control. Usually when no one was talking near her, her mind could be quiet. For her to count within her own memory…she was on edge. The last time she did it, she ended up in the hospital for a few days and had all her meds tripled in dosage. The hospital, with its tan, foam-lined walls and constant surveillance, coupled with her inability to do anything but sit on a bed, almost destroyed her. *Though if it hadn't been for that stay, she wouldn't have met Marissa.* Regardless, she never wanted to go back there. Never! And especially not because of a loud mouth.

She was going to take a sick day tomorrow, but the

idea of quitting and never going back was gone. The only thought, the only thing in her head at all, was:

STOP HIM FROM TALKING. Eighteen letters. Four words. Eighteen letters. Four words.

The next day was long and filled with lots of driving, but it was productive and purposeful. The day after, Martha was tired, but she got up and followed her normal morning routine. Only the counting was different; it was only the eighteen letters and four words, over and over. She'd say the line, count the letters and words, and move about on autopilot as she got ready for work before she left her apartment. Even when she got to her desk and saw the silicone rubber poop on her chair, even when she picked it up and all her co-workers laughed, even when loudmouth Franklyn came over and patted her on the back and sarcastically thanked her for cleaning up his mess, she just counted the words. *Eighteen letters.*

Martha didn't speak as everyone laughed. Ignoring them, she put on her headphones and started to work, yet every number she crunched ended up being eighteen. It was the only number she entered into every row and every column. By the time ten-fifteen rolled around, she'd written that beautiful number over two thousand times, destroying every accounting form she touched. It would only be a matter of days before others started to freak out when they saw every number was the same, but Martha, who prided herself on never getting a number wrong, didn't care. She had one thing to do today. One thing that was four words and eighteen letters long, and it was now time.

After Franklyn went out for his normal break, Martha waited a few minutes, then grabbed her purse and went out into the hallway. There were no nerves and no fear or panic; there were just the eighteen letters and four words running through her head over and over as she waited and watched the numbers above the elevator door dance from floor to floor. After counting the letters over a dozen times, the elevator stopped its dance, chimed softly, and the door opened. The three men inside were laughing heartily but stopped when they saw Martha. Then they broke out laughing even more.

"Franklyn, may I talk to you privately for a moment?" Martha asked, speaking out loud for the first time that day.

"Only if you washed your hands first," Franklyn said with a loud boisterous laugh that caused his buddies to bend over in hysterics. Martha showed not even the slightest facial reaction as they sauntered away. Franklyn stood in front of Martha, crossed his arms, and slowly stopped laughing.

"I know what you are going to say, but it was a joke and I do appreciate you cleaning up that mess, okay? No need to put in any complaints to HR. And besides, if you did, you know they'd side with me. So, what's the point, right? You do good work. Just keep doing it and we'll be fine." There were a lot of letters there, but Martha did not count them. Instead, she carefully reached into her purse and pulled out a thick manila envelope. Without a word, she held it out to Franklyn, who was starting to look a bit concerned. He eyed the envelope, but didn't touch it.

"What is that? You aren't serving me a lawsuit or something, are you? Because I'm telling you, if you even think about that, I will destroy your ass. You won't be able to find a job anywhere, you'll..." Martha looked him dead in the eyes, flared her nose, and spoke in a voice that she never heard come out of her mouth before.

"Open this now!" she said, instantly feeling a bit of gratification at the sight of fear seeping into Franklyn's face. He ripped the folder out of her hand, tore off the top, and pulled out the paper inside with clear anger. Martha watched the color drain from his face as he looked at one sheet after another...and the counting stopped in her head.

"This...these are lies. How did you even...I don't understand?" Franklyn said in a whisper as he quickly looked around the hall.

"Franklyn, on your first day, I knew exactly the type of person you were. I minored in advanced psychology. Men like you get away with a lot, but once in a while you push too hard. When you push the wrong domino over, they all fall. It wasn't hard to dig into your past. My girlfriend does research for a living. It was simple to find women you'd belittled and...worse. Men like you might not like me, but scorned women do. It was easy to get them to talk and they couldn't have signed these statements quicker." Martha was speaking like a courtroom prosecutor, with a sense of pride and conviction she'd never had.

"Martha...come on, please! I have a family. I have two daughters. You can't do this to me. It would destroy them. Think of them, please. If these, these lies, got out, it would...I can't imagine."

Hearing Franklyn speak, a smile finally crossed her face. "Oh Franklyn, the letters are a backup plan."

Franklyn looked confused; he scrunched up his face and shook his head.

"Look inside the envelope. There's something else." Martha watched as he looked inside the envelope. Sweat started to form on his head. The way his eyes widened filled her with a joy so deep she almost squealed with happiness.

"What am I supposed to do with that?" Franklyn asked in a low whisper. Martha poked her tongue out as far as she could and waved it back and forth. Franklyn shoved the envelope and papers back at Martha. She let them drop.

"There is something else you can cut off..." Martha said, looking down at his crotch. This time she didn't laugh. Franklyn put his hands on his head, turned around, and paced.

"You have until after lunch to decide. Make it look like some sort of accident. You just bit down too hard. Think of the sympathy you'll get! Or...lose your family, have multiple court cases, go bankrupt, and possibly spend the next few decades in jail wishing you'd used that little razor blade. It's your choice. I was very clear to all the women what your options would be. They all agreed that your tongue was a good price to pay." As Martha finished, she quickly turned and started to walk away. She could hear Franklyn coming up behind her, so she spun around and spoke quickly and loudly.

"Those are just copies on the floor. Five copies, one to your wife, are in an outgoing mail box in a location only I know. The mail gets picked up at 1:30. If I hear your voice after 1:25, I guess the copies get shipped out." Franklyn stopped and looked at her, and then spewed out exactly one-hundred and twenty-four letters of profanity.

***

The next two weeks at work without Franklyn were silent and peaceful and wonderful. She was able to blame the "accident" that happened for her mess-up on the accounting forms. They even gave her a few days off and she enjoyed every second of them with Marissa, even though that went against their routine. When he came back to work that third week, the entire floor applauded and shook hands with him. There were flowers and cards on his desk. The sympathy he received was enormous.

Once everyone settled down, Franklyn stood at his desk and wrote on a small whiteboard he held in his hands. After a few seconds of silence, he held it up for everyone to read: *Thank you. Now get to work!* Laughter erupted and Martha did just that. She got back to work and enjoyed the silence.

Swan Song

Jackson tried—he tried so damn hard, every day of his life—to be what *they* wanted him to be. Everything he did was calculated and carefully planned to ensure the best outcomes, which meant that he looked good in the end. The reason he tried so hard was because he didn't understand the rest of the world, or as he liked to call them, Humans. He felt so different and disconnected from them that he certainly could not be one. On the outside he was like a gameshow host, smiling and constantly putting on a show for everyone to see—and most ate it up. He was charming, personable, and almost every person that met him would talk about how damn good of a guy Jackson was. They were all fooled—all but one.

There was nothing intricately bad with Jackson; in fact, he'd like to think he didn't have a bad bone in his body. Whether the reasons behind his actions were shallow or real, he truly did everything he said and all his kind actions were real. What everyone didn't know, though, was that Jackson did these things because he didn't know how to act otherwise. There was no need or urge to be kind and funny or for him to follow every rule and law to the T. No, he did them because he observed humans and saw what was right and how people wanted others to act. It was as simple as that. His entire life and everything he did, he did as if following a script called "The Guide to Being a Good Person," which was probably written in 1955.

The odd part was that Jackson himself never knew he did this; he really thought he was good and kind. Yes, he had some emotions, but they were miniscule and different than those of most other humans. There were a lot of times where he simply didn't understand things or how people acted or why they felt things. Well, it was more than a lot; it was a constant. In those times, he simply observed those people and mimicked the emotions that he thought they needed or wanted to see. And that was how Jackson stumbled through life: as a perpetual actor who was never allowed to leave the stage. Then, one rainy day, inside of a cool and empty movie theater where he enjoyed a matinee alone, he saw a woman sitting alone…and everything changed.

In the flickering blue light of the screen, he noticed a curvy woman sitting up straight in her chair, a large popcorn on her lap. She was alone and had a lush head of curly hair that changed colors as the screen flashed through a technicolor make-believe world. Normally he would just check out a woman then go back to the movie, but she was doing something he had never seen anyone do, other than himself. The woman was mimicking the crying on the screen. At first, he thought she was really crying, but then she stopped and her face glazed over with no emotion. Then she tried on another empathetic face. One after another, she tried on various crying faces, oblivious that Jackson was staring at her.

Halfway through the movie, which was some blood-soaked action film with a horror undertone, the woman finally noticed he was staring. Instead of casually glimpsing him, she stared at him until he smiled and turned away. Jackson only snuck quick glances from then on, but they were still enough that, during the climax of the film, the woman stood up, walked over, and sat right next to him.

"You're either a sicko, a rapist, autistic, or so stunned by my beauty you can't handle it. Either way, I have a knife in my hand, so if you try anything, I'll cut you, leave, and no one will ever know it was me. I bought my ticket with cash. So why are you staring at me?" Jackson couldn't believe what was happening; he had never met someone so blunt and bizarre before. Normally he would lie about why and what he was doing, but looking at her, something told him to speak the truth.

"You. You were mimicking the emotions on the film. I have never seen anyone do that, except for myself."

The woman smiled and nodded towards the screen. "Let's finish the movie. We can talk after." Even a year later, on the night that would change his life forever, he could not recall the ending of that film. His heart was pounding too fast and hard to pay attention to the generic explosions and fights on the screen.

After the movie, they talked in the seats, where he learned her name was Rose, until they were kicked out. Then in the lobby, then the food court, then at the local Chili's, then in the parking lot until two in the morning.

Even then, after nine hours of talking and sharing secrets, they did not want to leave each other. For Jackson, it was like talking to someone from his own species for the first time, one he did not have to pretend with, one he did not have put on a show for or act a certain way around. It felt real and insanely amazing and he didn't want it to end, but they were still strangers and needed to say goodnight, so after a long hug, they did just that...then texted each other five minutes later and for another three hours until the sun started to come up. The next day, they texted each other from the jobs they both held just to keep appearances and pay bills; she was an advertising consultant at a local billboard company and he was a nurse at a local walk-in clinic (where patients waited longer than normal that day). They saw each other again that night and every night after. There'd only been a mere six nights in the next four months they were not together, and every second of it was pure bliss for Jackson.

Turning off the "show" versions of Jackson was like breathing for the first time. It was also like meeting a stranger, as he didn't even know himself. It only took a few days before they discussed "what" they both were; sociopaths, narcissistic, autistic, evolved, damaged, broken, lost, and countless other terms and ideas were thrown out to figure out why they both didn't feel human emotions the way the rest of the world did. In the end, they just decided to call themselves *The Others*, based off their mutual love of the film of the same name, even if the context was a bit off.

***

His entire life, he felt what he thought were "emotions," but in reality, they were nothing more than part of his act. Jackson was just another unknowing viewer of his show. Caught up in his own game, he thought he had emotions, but he was just mimicking what he thought he should do in every situation in his life. With Rose, for the first time in his life, he felt things that were new and he truly believed were real. They were powerful and amazing. Within two weeks, he knew he would do anything to keep her in his life.

Jackson gave her everything he had. He took the largest knife he had, cut open his chest, and showed his real insides, every dark and twisted turn inside of him. He let her examine without restrictions. Rose, on the other hand, while an intense and wonderful listener, only shared tiny nuggets. If he gutted himself for her to see, she merely used a pin and pricked the tiniest hole to peak through. Part of her was coy about why and teased that she needed to leave parts of her unknown so he could always desire and want more...and it worked. He wanted more; in fact, he could not get enough. When they started making love, Jackson cried, but Rose just looked at him with a look of peace and wonder, like someone watching a rainbow for the first time.

Looking back on the quick, hot, and intense three months, Jackson realized how oblivious he was. While he thought they were The Others, in reality, he was no different than a teenage girl who falls for the older guy who uses her for sex and companionship before throwing her aside when he was done. He was oblivious. With his hands covered in blood, and the police, seven in all, pointing guns at him, he realized it was all a setup. In his cell that night, he pondered if meeting Rose (which he learned was not her real name) in the theater was by chance or not. He decided it had to be—he'd researched her, after all—but he wouldn't have been surprised if it wasn't. Part of him was furious, but he did not once fall into the stereotypical screaming and yelling and kicking and punching of things, because that is what a human would do. Instead, he lay silently on the awfully lumpy cot and marveled at his stupidity and her genius ability to trick him.

What confused Jackson were the emotions. They were real to him for the first time ever. And she'd claimed they were for her as well. They'd connected on so many damn levels it had to have been real for her…but then he thought about all the women who had fallen in love with him. He'd treated them so damn good they thought he was Prince Charming and could do no wrong. When he got bored, he'd come up with a story as to why they had to end their love and they'd sob and sob, but still think he was wonderful. And they'd come back over and over again, anytime he wanted or needed sex, and every time they'd leave and still think he was an amazing guy. If he could do it to countless women…why couldn't Rose have done it to him? While furious and full of vengeance, he forced himself to be impressed instead of angry. And in reality, he still appreciated her because even if her side was fake, *he'd* felt stuff for the first time in his life and it was miraculous. It was like seeing a god you didn't think existed. There was no going back to being a disbeliever after that.

When he met with his public defender, Jackson was again impressed. There wasn't a damn trace of Rose anywhere. She was a visual ghost. No one fitting her description worked at the building he had picked her up at countless times. He always thought it was odd that she didn't let him take pictures, or the fact that she had no social media pages, but he'd shrugged it off, as he had other friends that were the same way about "Big Brother" and posts. He gave the lawyer over two dozen ways to find his Rose, but all of them came up empty. She'd even somehow skirted the security cameras at several of the places they frequented, a mere shoulder or elbow showing up in the footage like she was some highly trained spy who knew how to go unnoticed in public. When his defender mentioned going for an insanity plea, Jackson laughed out loud.

"Jackson, I know this is hard, but this woman doesn't exist. One bartender even said he remembered you eating alone several times at Chili's, the place where you said you guys ate together every week. You made her up. If we can show the judge that you had delusions of another person who made you kill that couple, then we can get you a sentence in a mental hospital. It would be a lot better there and maybe...maybe you'll get some help." Jackson did get mad at this. He might have been tricked and fooled, but he was not crazy and no one was going to tell him he was. The bartender had to have been paid off. Rose was real… right?

That night he really did go crazy, racking his brain trying to figure out if maybe he did hallucinate Rose. *Was she real? It felt so damn real. People had to have seen them together. What the fuck?* His mind splintered into two halves going back and forth: *real, not real, tricked, trick of the mind, fact, fiction, fantasy, reality.* Everything hurt. It was a tug of war in his brain for hours and days. In the end, he started to think she was not real, because how could such a perfect woman, who was the mirror image of himself, be real? It wasn't possible to have such perfection and wonder in life and not ruin it. They make movies about the ultimate love story, but they were nothing compared to their connection. It was them versus the world and they were the only ones that mattered…something that magical couldn't have been real. Part of him desperately wanted her to be, though, because he wanted to feel the way he made her feel once again. Hell, he'd kill ten more people to feel that one more time.

***

The months went by, no new evidence was found, and the trial finally came. Against everyone's wishes and a few injunctions by the state claiming he was insane, Jackson turned down all counsel, fired his lawyer, and asked to represent himself. He had fooled people his entire life and now was his last chance—one *swan song,* you could say—where he could get up and make the twelve jurors believe him. If they believed, like he did, that Rose was real, they'd let him go; they'd understand he killed those people because they had abused and raped the love of his life when she was a teenager; they'd understand he did it out of pure love and passion and revenge and that they deserved what they got, because the justice system failed back then…don't let it fail again now.

With a big smile on his face, he stood up for his opening statement, put on the full Game Show Host mask he always wore, and started to speak. Turning to the jurors, sitting there just like a studio audience, he felt his nerves bubble with excitement. This was going to be one hell of a show. Opening his mouth to speak, a tiny movement in the back of the courtroom caught his eye. One of the studio audience stood up; she wore glasses, her hair was different, and she had a painted-on mole that wasn't there before, but he instantly knew it was Rose. She merely smiled at him, gave him a nod, and sat back down…she was eager for the show to begin. Jackson understood it all then. He had to win this trial; it was all a test. If he won, he'd prove himself to Rose as worthy and she'd come back.

Be Mine

Without you, the world is less divine
Be mine, Be mine…

Rose tore up the poem before even finishing reading half of its sickening lines. The paper was deep red and was some expensive stock so she had to put some effort into tearing it into the amount of pieces she wanted. Tossing it into the trash, she went to the next one with a sigh. Looking at the stack, she shook her head; there had to be forty more. Rose had to close her eyes and take a deep breath to calm herself. The hunt was always exhausting, but more than worth it—she just had to remind herself of that at times. After exactly seventeen more letters, more than half with shitty poems either made up or stolen from some website, she found the one for the year. It was on normal paper, handwritten (which was rare these days), and simply vulgar. Of course, it had a poem as well:

Once you feel how I lick,
You will scream for my dick

Sometimes it was just too easy. Twenty years ago, she had to work a bit harder at this, but with the internet and dozens of dating sites, she had more than her pick of men for her yearly Valentine's party.

Every year she picked a new name. This year it was Rose, in honor of it being her twentieth year playing this game. She'd actually saved the name all these years for a special occasion, and this anniversary was it. There wasn't much of a reason behind it, as it was just a name she'd always loved, so when she used it, she wanted it to be special—and getting away with the game for two decades was certainly special.

Once the name was picked, she would then create the fake profile (depending on her mood, she would do one to four social media sites) and post a pic of herself. It was always a real picture, but never her real hair or the way she wore her makeup, and she would usually add a beauty mark or fake contacts and almost always use some sort of "cute" filter. But it really had to be her; if not, when she met them or if they asked for proof that she was not some fake profile, they wouldn't believe her. Trust was important. Dressing up and taking the pictures was one of the parts she actually enjoyed. It helped her create the character to go with the name. Once she had on the creamy skin-toned lipstick, auburn wig, and green contacts, with a splatter of light freckles, she became Rose—but who *was* Rose? That first day, standing in the mirror, Rose became a divorced mother of one. Looking at how sexy she was all made up, she decided that Rose couldn't have a menial job. She had to be successful and smart. She was too damn attractive to be a nobody. A professor seemed perfect, but she instantly knew that would cut her pool of men by more than half—men hated a woman too smart or successful—so a third-grade teacher with a master's in education it was. Men always loved the idea of role playing with a teacher.

The profile was always posted in late December with a story about how she was "starting fresh" for the new year, freshly divorced, new page with maiden name! The men always went crazy for divorced women as they were typically "horny" after being with one man for so long—at least that is what she was told over and over again. Without fail, within two hours of posting, she would have numerous DMs saying a casual "hello" from complete strangers. *All* of them men. The first time she received a dick pic with no words and no context, she was shocked. Now, she expected them, even if she didn't understand the mass volume of men who would just randomly send a picture of their cock without ever talking. Outside of her hunting season (Dec-Feb), she would take all these pics, match them to the profile, and do a little detective work. If they had wives or children, she sent them the picture along with any explicit messages that came with it. If they didn't have family, she posted the pics on DickWall.org, a dick-pic-shaming site. Of course, she would then send the posting to the man to let them know that their unwanted picture was now being seen my millions.

Some days her hunting was exhausting, other times it was thrilling. However, there was no way around it: it was work. Lots of work. Going through profiles, responding to dozens of men back and forth daily, and carefully researching each one to find the perfect few was a full-time job. Rose never purposely set out on this journey and in fact never dreamed of doing what she did; however, it happened, and what started as an accident led to an obsession that she promised she would only be once a year. Then she bent that rule by keeping it to "once" a year timewise, but multiple men instead of just one like she did the first five years. With it being the twentieth anniversary, she couldn't help but look back at all that had happened.

Twenty years ago, when her husband died after sniffing a line of bad coke off a stripper's ass in a club, she had no clue her mild-mannered life would lead here. Of course, she knew he went to the strip club and it didn't bother her. What did bother her was the scandal that followed his death. The day after he died, the local newspaper and eventually the national news reported the headline "Beloved High School Teacher Dies Sniffing Cocaine Off Former Student's Body at Strip Club." Embarrassment, shame, anger, and countless similar words did not do her emotions justice. Besides losing the love of her life, she'd found out all sorts of things about the man she loved, his secret life of drugs and talking students into becoming strippers, and his personal sex slaves. Nine girls went on record after saying they'd gotten into stripping because of the money he promised. They'd talked about how he "groomed" them, yet he never broke a law, nor did he touch them until they graduated and were working as strippers. However, once they stripped, he was their "pimp" of sorts and made them give him a percentage of their earnings for protecting them, and getting them the job in the first place.

The media had a field day and kept researching and finding out more, though Rose knew half of them were just strippers looking for their five minutes of fame. Every day, someone was at her door. There had been hundreds of requests for interviews; it was exhausting and terrifying, but she did not break down and never made a single statement. Instead, she packed up and left at two in the morning with what little she needed. She used an auction firm to sell her house and everything in it and started a new life. With the money from the house, her husband's car, and the life insurance, she had freedom to do what she wanted for the rest of her life. It was the one good thing he did. After settling six states away and using her maiden name, she took up a new life, but she was leery of men and didn't want them to find out who she was, and that was how she started her first fake profile online.

Within hours of that first online profile, she was being solicited by men, mostly married. The dick pics came fast and hard, no pun intended. The anger that was under her skin quickly rose to the surface. She truly just wanted to find a date; instead, married cock after married cock sent her pictures. The anger she had was oppressive. Anger at her husband, at his friends, the media, but mostly at herself for not knowing what the fuck was happening with her own love and best friend. She needed to relieve some stress and wanted to use someone like these men wanted to use her, so she bought a wig and agreed to a date with Timothy Lamont, thirty-three, who said he was single. In reality, he had three kids and a wife of over ten years. It took her all of ten minutes to figure that out. His stupidity amazed her at the time, but she quickly got use to men being really, really dumb any time blood flowed below the belt.

When she met Timothy at a Chili's bar two towns over (she was not oblivious to his choosing of the town), she was pleasantly surprised. He was a good-looking man and friendly, but most of all, she loved that she laughed with him. The hours passed quickly, and while he drank heavily, she monitored her intake to make sure she had full ability of her thinking. If she didn't know he was married, it would have been a perfect date. When he suggested they go somewhere quiet to "hang out," she was a bit naive and didn't realize he meant a hotel. When he showed her the room key, she realized he'd planned this all out and only had one motive. His profile said "looking for the one," but a pre-booked room in a fuck motel was not looking for love. The feeling was crushing. Part of her wanted to believe that maybe he was just in a horrible marriage and wanted a reason to get out of it, but instead, he was just another man who wanted someone to fuck on the side.

Looking at the key half hidden under the cocktail napkin as if it were some sort of drug he was showing her he had, she took a deep breath and tried to decide what to do. It was then she realized she was pretending to be someone else as well, so why not? He was good-looking and she could use some intimacy. Maybe she would be the one to use someone for once. With a simple nod, he paid the bill and they slipped outside. She followed him in her car to the hotel and, of course, he parked at the back door that was "for guests only" where no one except another guest would see his vehicle. Before she got out of the car, she checked to make sure she had her mace and her hand spike she could use to stab with in case this turned into something else. Knowing it was by her side, she followed him through the door and down the hall to the last room on the right.

Once inside, he kicked off his shoes and told her to put her purse down, so she carefully placed it on the nightstand, which was awkward as it took up all the free space, but she didn't care. She had never done anything like this and only dated traditionally, so she was a bit nervous and didn't know how to start, but it didn't matter. He took charge by walking over and kissing her hard on the mouth. It felt good—really good. Within seconds, they were naked and he was on top of her. All thoughts of her fake name and his lies were gone. Just pure physical lust and desire wrestled on the bed.

When it was over, he hardly wasted time getting into the bathroom to wash up. When he came back out, he was half dressed and checking his phone. There was some sort of half-assed excuse before he kissed her, apologized, and left, telling her to "feel free to stay in the room if she wanted." The night had been wonderful until that moment. Part of her had even been wondering if maybe they would fall in love and reveal the truth to each other, but it was all ripped apart in that moment. As he turned to walk away, she said, "Cathy will know before you're home." Timothy stopped in his tracks, his shoulders slumped. Rose sat up and stuck her hand in the bag, not knowing if he would snap and attack her.

"What the fuck did you say?" Tim said, turning around dramatically as if ready for his close-up in a film's finale.

"I documented all our talks. I took pictures of you tonight when you were not looking; you didn't notice because your face was buried between my legs, but the tattoo of Darth Vader on your shoulder is very clear and distinct." She could see him start to tremble as he sat down in the desk chair across from her.

"What…what is this? What do you want?" Rose was not expecting this; in fact, she had no clue what she was expecting.

"I want you to be mine." The words came out of her mouth without any thought or knowing what she meant, and by the look on his face, he had no clue as well. That was how the game started. From that day forward, she used Timothy like a puppet. If she wanted sex, she made him pay for a room and show up exactly when she wanted or else… And if she wanted to buy anything, it was his job to buy it. At first, she didn't know what she was doing or why, but it quickly became fun and an obsession. The more hoops he jumped through, the more she wanted to push to see how far he would go. At times he would throw a fit and protest and fight and refuse, to which she would just say, "OK then, have fun tonight when she gets the photos." Then he would do whatever she said.

When the normal stuff like gifts and sex got boring, the darkness she never knew she had started to creep out. She'd make Tim take pictures of himself masturbating in the dressing room at Kohls while his wife shopped for him. She made him wear her used underwear to work one day, made him eat his own semen that dripped out of her, and even pissed on him fully clothed, which resulted in him having to pay a hefty cleaning bill at the hotel.

For a while he thought it was slightly fun getting to have sex and have a woman bossing him around, but then he quickly got pissed and the sex got a bit rough to the point she feared for her safety. That was when she decided it was time to end things. With a quick text, she made him meet him at the hotel; she told him to get undressed and to sit in the chair. Thankfully he did not protest when she tied him up, though of course it helped that she said she wanted to apologize and give him the best blowjob he ever had. When he was tied up, she got on her knees, leaned towards his hard cock, then slapped it hard and laughed.

"You're an idiot." Getting up, she pulled out a folder and started to show him all the printouts of their texts and conversations. She even put together a spreadsheet of all the things he bought her, which were worth thousands of dollars. The pictures of them screwing pissed him off the most. She simply said it was amazing how small hidden cameras were nowadays.

Carefully, she laid it all out as he yelled and yelled at her about what the fuck she was doing. When she was satisfied at how it all looked, she took his phone, used his thumb against his will to open it, and texted his wife that there was an emergency and to come get him in room 167 at the Claremont Inn.

The moment she left, Rose pulled off the fake nails, stopped in a bathroom and washed off the makeup she didn't wear in her normal life, plucked off the fake mole, and slipped out of the hotel. An hour later, after she deleted all the accounts associated with her fake persona, the woman Tim had been tortured by no longer existed. Part of her thought she was panicking, but she quickly realized it was not panic...it was adrenaline coursing through her. She desperately wanted to be a fly on the wall to see how it played out and what the wife's reactions would be to finding him that way, but alas...all she could do was monitor his social media from afar. It was only a month later when his status changed to single.

What amazed her the most was that she felt no guilt. There was no way she would ever feel it for Tim, as his actions had caused what happened, but his poor wife and family... She tried and tried but she simply felt nothing for them. After a lot of thinking, she told herself it was because they were better off without him. In the weeks that followed what happened, she couldn't stop thinking about it. She loved the power and thrill of what she had done. She wanted to do it again...soon. With her new life on track and from fear of getting caught, she decided to use the fun as a treat to herself by making it a once-a-year thing, like a yearly "vacation" you might say. And so, her Valentine's day hunt began. Year after year, she'd find the perfect sleaze ball, let them seduce her, and then blackmail and torture them. Some years there were more than one; some men she was harder on and a few she let out of her grasp without any punishment. She never got caught (only a few close calls), though she got physically hurt four times, but they got theirs tenfold and have scars to always remember her by. She moved around and spread her web further to keep things safe. Though no matter what, the game gave her more fulfillment and sense of self-worth than anything else she had ever had in her life.

***

With the twentieth anniversary here, Rose thought about how spectacular it was going to be, but she also felt a bit of melancholy. Sipping a subtle white wine, scrolling through the computer to make sure everything was in place, she thought about how different things would be this year, especially since she was about to hit fifty. Part of her felt more powerful and sexier the closer she got to the age that scared most women. In a way, she felt like a sexual superhero that got her powers from destroying men. She liked thinking of herself as a vigilante. After all, she got vengeance for women everywhere by screwing men over, just like they screwed women. When this was all over, women around the world would praise her, she would get a seven-figure book deal; hell, life would be…*thump*… The noise did more than shock her. She had lived alone for over twenty years; not even a pet kept her company. A noise that loud, near her back door after ten at night…her heart sank, knowing what it had to be.

Within seconds, she had an old wooden bat she kept in the closet in her right hand, left hand the cell phone ready. There was another noise, this one not as loud. Stepping in to her kitchen, her heart flipped as she saw the backyard motion light snap on. For half a second, she wished it was a racoon or some other nocturnal animal, but she saw the shadow of a man's frame. Using her finger, she swiped to unlock her phone and dial 911. The second she hit the 9, she saw a man walk right up to the back door. He was much older, scruffier, and grayer than she remembered. Time was not kind to him to say the least, but there was no doubt it was Timothy. This sudden realization made her finger hover over the 1. She could call and say she had never seen this man before. Twenty years had passed with no evidence that the persona Tim knew ever existed…she'd win any legal case. Besides, in reality, there was no crime she committed. She hit the 1 button, but then something hit her in the back of the head.

***

When she awoke, she was tied to a chair, eerily similar to how she left Tim all those years ago. Her head thumped over and over and her vision was a bit blurry, but the second she could open her eyes, she knew she was in trouble. There were six men standing around her, another two sitting on the couch…she knew every damn one of them. Without thinking, she blurted out, "Jonathan, please don't!" The men all looked around at each other as if to see which one was John, but no one seemed to respond. Timothy then walked into the room, smiling and looking a bit cocky. A stocky man with a crooked nose—Rose could not recall his name—nodded to Tim and then chuckled to himself.

"Well, looks like things finally have caught up to you, whore." Rose thought the line was funny; these guys snuck around and fucked everything that would spread its legs and she was the whore? She couldn't help but smile, but it was then she could see how pissed it made a few of them. She wondered what their plan was. Rape and beat her…or just kill her? Regardless of what they wanted, she had to play along.

"What…what is going on? I…I know I dated all of you, but I never meant to hurt any of you. Some of you I loved so much. Especially you, Timothy. Why, what do you want?" Her voice was shaking; she hoped she didn't put it on too thick. A few laughed at her question while a couple looked confused. A shorter guy, one she vaguely remembered being called Rick, ran up to her and slapped her hard. It hurt like fuck and was hard enough to cause blood to stream out of her nose. She started to cry, a little from the pain, but more so because she needed to act it up.

"Can we just skip to the part where we fuck her to death? I can't stand looking at this cunt." The man who said this was standing behind the couch. She couldn't see his face, but she recalled his voice. He was the one who always got…too rough. The one she suspected had killed before, the one she had to cut short the game on and actually move for her own safety. It was then that real fear set in and she had to end the game well before she wanted to.

"Jonathan! BE MINE!" Again, all the men seemed confused, especially the second all the lights snapped on and her computer screen lit up. Over half of them said, "What the fuck?" at the same time. One of them saw the camera in the corner of the room and pointed to it. They all started mumbling while two ran for the door.

"Ladies…these are the ones I was telling you about, the ones I feared for years would come to hurt me. I told you, I told you they would. These men are sick! Help, help! Any of you that are watching live, please call the police." Hearing that last line, they all started to run for the door… everyone except for Tim.

"You fucker, you thought of everything. All of this was a game from day one with one great finale in place."

Rose—well, that wasn't her name—forced down a smile and said, "Please, Tim…please don't hurt me." It was overdramatic and she winked with the eye facing away from the camera. It sent Tim into a rage, but just as he balled his fist, ready to kill, she whispered, "Adding assault to kidnapping and breaking and entering… I'd say you'll get at least thirty years." Tim's face turned purple; his eyes watered.

"Then I might as well go for a murder charge as well." Rose's heart sank. The wake code of "Be Mine" had started the live stream, so someone should have called the police immediately, but God knows how long they would take to get there. As Tim ran at her, screaming, snot dripping out of his nose, she sighed heavily, braced for the impact, and wondered if the game was truly over, or if she was going to get a book deal by the end of the week.

Pulse

Waaathump. Waaathump. Waaathump. The sound was deafening. Three long sounds, each with a high-pitched wind-up followed by a booming, thumping noise. It was like a giant was screeching before slamming a massive club down on the earth, shaking the ground with the power of an aftershock. Each whaling pulse lasted a total of six seconds, with a ten-second pause in between them. The first time the earth shook was such a visceral experience that it caused utter chaos in the school. Everyone screamed out different theories about what was happening...everyone except for Marcus Newman. He knew *exactly* what the noise was: a signal for him to take action.

As a textbook loser with no friends, high school was a stereotypical hell for Marcus. Being overweight and acne prone with bad hair and poor clothing choices didn't help his case, though Marcus didn't even attempt to fit in. If he learned anything from movies, all he had to do was wait until school was over and he'd have a fresh start in college, the elite ones that all the popular kids were too dumb to get into. Then he'd start on the path to creating some sort of app or invention that would make him millions. Then he could hire the jocks to mow his lawn, deliver his food, and drive him to events. Every time a spit ball hit him, or he was shoved in the hall or teased in the locker room, he made a mental note to lower the percent of the tip he would give these idiots for their future mundane services. While he always expected the signal, he truly hoped he would never hear the call. When the "thumping" started, he knew all future plans were canceled for good. There would be no tips for anyone.

The first one shook the school when he was ironically in AP Science, listening to a lecture on the tectonic plates. Everyone screamed when their desks rattled on the scratched-up linoleum… everyone except his teacher, who looked excited and started to yell about how they were experiencing science firsthand. Students clamored to get under their desks and fought for a space in the doorframe like they were all taught to do during earthquake drills. Marcus on the other hand got up, grabbed his bag, and pushed his way out of the door, right through two girls who were about to rip each other's hair out to be the one to stand in the safety of the steel frame like they were taught. Walking down the hallway in a hurry, he listened to the screams and watched the small puffs of ceiling tile dust fall. He had to get home.

Leaving on his own, there was no bus to take. The long walk home was exhausting for Marcus; he cursed the rule about juniors not being allowed to drive cars to school. It was almost in the nineties, and with his black jeans and matching polo, he was sweating and chafing in places he didn't know he could, but he ignored it and pushed through the pain and exhaustion. Three miles later, with blisters, heat rashes, and soaked clothing, he burst into his house, sucked down two bottles of water, stuck his head in the freezer, then got to work. Thankfully, his parents wouldn't be home for hours. It would give him time to prepare and pack up to leave before they arrived. Grabbing his worn dog-eared copy of Jack Steinman's *When They Arrive*, the mass market edition with the earth cracking open and orange light spilling out on the cover, Marcus started to nod. He had known since he was twelve, when he first read the book, that it was *not* fiction—not at all. It was a warning.

Jack Steinman was a genius, no doubt about that. Not many fiction writers had two PhDs. Marcus read everything the man ever wrote, watched every interview Jack ever did online, and knew everything about the writer, right down to what the man ate for breakfast. When Marcus got his license and a beat-up old sedan for his sixteenth birthday, the first thing he did was take a four-hour drive to Maryland to see Jack's mansion on the coast. He sat there for hours staring at the house, eating junk food and pissing in a bottle, hoping for a glimpse of the man, but no one ever left the house. In the past year, he had gone down five more times to just sit and watch. On the last trip, the prophet himself came out to grab his mail.

When Marcus saw Jack, the gray hair and slender body he had seen in so many interviews and author photos, he froze, stopped breathing, then burst out of the car with orange cheese puff crumbs all over his chest and ran across the street. The man he adored jumped back and put his hands up, so Marcus did the same to show him he meant no harm, exposing his sticky, neon, tangerine-colored fingers. Marcus then blurted out some long rambling speech about how he was his biggest fan and that he read between the lines and cracked his code, that he understood, truly understood, what he was trying to tell everyone. The man kept backing up, but Marcus kept approaching him. When Jack told him the work was just fiction, Marcus watched the man's eyes as they looked around; understanding they were being watched, he couldn't tell the truth in broad daylight. Marcus nodded to him and gave him a wink.

The next time he drove down, a police officer arrived a mere five minutes after he'd parked and harassed him, told him to get out of town and to never come back again or else he'd be arrested. Marcus laughed in the man's face; the government coverup was ridiculous and blatant. They must have had Jack under extensive surveillance. Poor Jack had been petrified the day they first met, so they must have been watching him and worried that Marcus would expose his secrets. Taking one last glance at the mansion before pulling away, he saw that one of the upstairs window curtains was halfway down, but all the rest in the house were wide open. It was just like in *When They Arrive* when the main character signals for help after being held hostage. Marcus understood what he had to do: he had to prepare, and when the signal came, he would save Jack Steinman.

When the sounds started three days later, he knew

it was all connected and that it was the moment the books told him to look for. Laying the paperback on the comforter, he pulled out rolled up sheets of paper from under his bed and spread them out next to the book. Marcus had to look one more time to be sure he was reading the messages right. One by one, he checked the first letter of the first line in each chapter in the book to the sheet of paper to ensure he had them all correct. *He did.* While the letters were originally all jumbled, once he decoded them, the message was clear. *When it sounds, kill those who stand in your way and save me.*

Marcus felt tingles of anticipation and nerves rush through his body like a thousand racecars seeing who could run the track the fastest. This was the moment he was ready for but that he also dreaded. Part of him always knew this day would come, that it would start with the signal first, but the other part of him feared what would happen after it began. Lost in thought, his body trembled as he contemplated how life was supposed to be. Lost in a fantasy, a light knock on the door made him jump like a startled cat. Grabbing his papers, he rolled them as fast as he could, screaming for whoever was at his door to hold on, but the door opened anyway.

"Marcus, what is going on? The school called and said you were the only student who didn't come back after the tremors. I had to leave work, sweetie." His mother, who was always so soft-spoken, asked in a near whisper. Turning around, red faced and now shaking, he looked at his mother, who looked so much like him, just older and with longer hair.

"Didn't you hear it? The sound, the vibration? It's happening, Mom. I have to do something," Marcus exclaimed with wavering passion. Catching his breath, he watched as his mother took a big sigh before putting a hand on her chest and speaking again.

"Are you taking your meds, Marcus?" *The meds question.* Every time he said anything she didn't like or if he was the slightest bit cranky or annoyed or anything other than the perfect son, she'd ask that cruel question. And every damn time it infuriated him. Swallowing hard, he was about to scream at her that he was taking it every day, even though he wasn't, but at that very moment, the sound started again.

Waaathump. Waaathump. Waaathump

Marcus and his mother both steadied themselves, but neither fought for the doorframe nor ran outside. As the sounds settled, Marcus started to cry before looking at his mother.

"See, Ma…this is it." Marcus sobbed with a hitch in his voice. His mother just watched him as he grabbed a backpack and stuffed the papers and books inside.

"That noise is scary, sweetie, but it's probably the fracking or something; they were starting that soon." Marcus didn't respond. He ignored her as he turned to leave the room, but she was standing in the doorway, her arms crossed, her full round hips touching each side of the wood frame.

"You can't leave, Marcus, you're having an…" Marcus heard the line screamed at him inside of his head, *Kill those who stand in your way*. He was far from in shape, but he had youth, adrenaline, and height on his mother. Using both hands, he put his palms out flat and pushed her as hard as he could. The second his palms touched her shirt, he realized the cellar door, which sat across from his room, was wide open, like Dad always left it for the cat.

For being a large woman, she flew backwards with ease. If the door had been shut, she would have merely slammed into it and stayed on her feet, but it wasn't, and instead she stumbled down steep gray wood stairs…backwards. Marcus watched in horror as his mother twisted and contorted down the hard steps, her head and face slamming rough edges until she finally lay still in an unnatural pile that made his stomach turn. He couldn't breathe. He wanted to scream and cry and help her and call for an ambulance so she could be better and hold him like she always did when he couldn't take it all, but then the sounds came again. *Waaathump. Waaathump. Waaathump.* He had to keep going. With one last glance down at her crumpled, unmoving body, he whispered he was sorry and raced for his car.

The ride was excruciatingly long and hot. Marcus wanted to hear the signals as he drove, so he kept the music and air conditioner off and left the window open. With the wind whipping in, it was hard to determine if he was hearing the noise or if the loud sounds were something else off in the distance. After half an hour on the road, he didn't hear anything but traffic sounds, which made his stomach knot, for he could be too late.

The code he'd deciphered in the book was clear, but it didn't give specifics. If he didn't make it in time, he would never be able to forgive himself.

A little over halfway through the drive, his car started to ding, and the little red gas light came on. Marcus slammed his hand against the wheel and held back tears. He should have known to always keep his car ready. Getting off the highway and stopping could lose him valuable minutes, but he had no choice. Cutting across traffic, he raced off the first exit and sped to the orange sign that declared it sold gas. Cramming the nozzle in his car, he darted inside where he found a line of six people waiting. Holding a twenty in his fist, he felt like an imaginary hand had reached out and grasped him and started to squeeze. The crushing pain in his chest felt real, like there was an invisible monster trying to kill him. It was much stronger than his normal panic attacks; it had to be something more. It was getting hard to breathe and the room was blurry. Letting out a sobbing cry, almost everyone in line turned and looked at him. The second he saw their stoic faces filled with fake concern and shock, he knew they were all in on this. They were purposely standing there, taking their time to delay him, to stop him from getting to Jack's house before it happened.

"Screw all of you!" Marcus screamed with snot pouring out of his nose. Rushing back to his car, he saw the old woman parked in front of him pull back her credit card and put it in her wallet as she started to fill her tank. Getting in his car, he started it up, hit the gas, and slammed into the woman's car. The lady screamed and ran out of his view. Pushing as hard as he could on the gas, his wheels started to spin and burn, sending up a noxious cloud of black smoke, but it worked. The car in front of him was moving. After thirty seconds of the metallic shoving match, he was far enough forward to reach the gas pump. Jumping out, he pulled out the nozzle from his pump, which had snapped off and grabbed the woman's out of her tank. Before his tank was filled, a crowd had grown, cautiously watching from a distance, half of them filming on their phones for their followers online and hoping something would explode so they could have a viral video.

With his tank full, he pulled out the nozzle and turned towards the gathering group and pulled the trigger. No one was close enough to get splashed, but it got the reaction he wanted: they all ran away. Spraying everything he could with gas, he threw the nozzle down on the ground, got into his car, and pushed the cigarette lighter in. Backing out, he faced his car in the right direction, grabbed the lighter, and threw it out his window before hitting the gas. Marcus felt a tingle of excitement as he waited for the gas station to explode as he drove off, like some epic slow-motion scene in an action film, but nothing happened. As he looked in his rear-view mirror, all he saw was flashing blue lights in the distance.

Marcus was not the best driver in the world, but the adrenaline rocketing through his veins and the need to save Jack Steinman made him keep his foot to the accelerator and his hands on the wheel. Even when the one cop car became four and then ten, even when the helicopter started to follow, he focused and drove the last hour to Jack's house. Every time he avoided a roadblock or magically swerved around the spike strips, he knew fate was on his side, rooting for him against corruption.

When he was ten minutes away from his destination, the real panic set in. It was the moment of truth. Heading through the residential neighborhood at speeds over ninety miles an hour, Marcus took a deep breath and skyrocketed through the cross street and right through the Steinman's fence, which ripped apart like it was made out of Lincoln Logs. As the tires ripped apart the lawn, making its pathway to the house, Marcus knew he was going to make it. Three massive bumps and a slam later, his car smashed through the entryway of the house, though his head was bleeding from slamming into the steering wheel. Part of him wished he had airbags, but he also knew if he did, they would have gone off back at the gas station, stopping his mission right then and there.

Stumbling out of the car, climbing over the debris, he turned and looked through the demolished wall to see the police surrounding the house with caution. It didn't matter, though; he'd made it inside. Wiping his face to get the blood out of his eyes, he surveyed the room, wondering which way to go. Common sense told him an office would be upstairs and the most logical place

Steinman would be. Sprinting up the grand white staircase, Marcus had a hard time keeping his balance, almost falling. He had to grip the railing hard. At the top of the stairs, he looked around. The house was insane. The landing area at the top of the staircase could fit his entire house.

There were three doors off of the large open area of the landing and he could see more down each side of the hall. Just when he decided he would have to search each one, he heard a voice in his head tell him, *the middle door*. A smile spread across his face. His brain was starting to sync with Jack's; they were getting a psychic connection as he got closer, just like Fred Whitmore in *The Stars Explode*. Marcus knew everything in the books was true. Grabbing the ornate silver handle, he pushed the door open to reveal…a bathroom. Marcus shook his head, confused. Pressure was building in his skull. The voice clearly said the middle one. Ignoring that he was wrong, he raced to the second door and opened it…a game room. The third, a bedroom.

In panic, he speed-walked, limping, to each door on the second floor, twelve in all, bursting into each room, hoping to find the office and Jack himself. As he opened the last door, a broom closet, the helicopter noise became deafening above the house and the pressure in his skull became worse. *The office had to be downstairs*. Stumbling, almost falling over his feet from pain, confusion, and exhaustion, Marcus clamored down the stairs before stopping in his tracks and letting out a guttural scream. There, under the car, was a leg…*a brown loafer and tan pants*. It wasn't moving.

As if someone snapped their fingers to shut off the world, the helicopter sound suddenly stopped and the sirens and commands being shouted through bullhorns ceased. Marcus could hear only his breathing, which was hitched and erratic. Walking down the last few steps, he walked to the mess on the floor, bent down, and touched the shoe lightly. *Finish my work*. The words were so clear in his head that he knew this time they couldn't be wrong, and he knew what he had to do.

Pulling out his phone, he went to the only site he visited regularly, *Steinman's Sentinels*, an underground fan site that discussed the truth in Jack's books, and made a post urging all the fans to watch his live feed. Switching over to his social media account, with all of its thirty-eight followers, he tapped the live feed button and pointed the camera at the leg under his car as he stated who the dead person was and how it was the government who'd killed the legendary writer and prophet. He ranted that the government knew he was coming, so they'd killed Jack and set him right in the spot they assumed he'd drive through to set him up, and he'd fallen for it. Marcus took the blame for doing exactly what they wanted, but he was in control now.

Walking through the downstairs of the mansion, he spewed conspiracies as the numbers watching his live stream went from single digits to double, then triple, before tens of thousands were watching him live by the time he finally found the office. The room where Jack wrote all of his stories was just as grand as he always thought it would be. Dark wood shelves, awards strewn about, framed articles and book covers. It was like walking into "God's own den," he stated to the people watching. Then there was the desk, which was bigger than his bedroom at home, carved out of some sort of black wood; it was perfection. Sitting down in the opulent leather chair, Marcus set up the camera against a box of cigars and spoke more before suddenly grabbing his head in pain.

Waaathump. Waaathump. Waaathump.

The signal was suddenly slamming inside of his skull, not just all around him. Tears streaming from his eyes, he screamed and asked if they could all hear it too. The small screen shot up random messages, some laughing, others mocking, but mixed in were thousands of people saying YES. They heard it. They could hear it, not just in his town, but all over the world. The secret was out; he had done it. Steinman had died for his cause, but it was not in vain, for the truth was set free.

"They did this. They have controlled us for too long. Steinman was warning us all these years through his books! Just read…" Marcus heard the crack a millisecond before the glass shattered and the hot sting raced through his skull. As he fell face first, the inside of his skull suddenly being exposed to his live stream, Marcus smiled, knowing they might have killed him, but it was too late. The world knew and they could all hear it now. *Waaathump. Waaathump. Thump…thum.*

Likes

"Seventeen... seventeen?" Candice dropped the phone on the bed, tears filling her eyes like a flashflood. Lying on her back, the tears pooled before spilling down her cheeks and running into her ears. For a brief moment, there was a thought of how gross and uncomfortable it was, but she then again thought of that god-awful number. *Seventeen.* Reaching over, she grabbed a tissue off the nightstand, blotted both eyes, and wiped each cheek. With a deep belly breath, Candice looked over to see if Sam was sleeping. Sure enough, he was still out, just like every night. It was three in the morning, after all. Two more breaths and she vowed to not check the phone again. It could wait until morning.

She checked it again at 4:13, then at 5:26. Still that nasty number: *seventeen.*

Candice's first words that morning were, "Get it yourself! You're ten years old, Gunnar. Christ!" She was screaming so loud on a dry morning throat that she instantly felt the damage; her voice would be hoarse all day. The two more hours of sleep she wanted—more so, *needed*—were not enough to stop the need to pick up her phone. Her stomach twisted. Candice tried to tell herself that it was just hunger, but deep down, she knew it was nerves. *Belly breaths.*

Picking up the phone, thumb on autopilot, she hit

the little blue square with the lowercase f. The little tiny bell in the bottom corner of the screen was moving back and forth silently to announce there were notifications. That was always a good sign, but the little red number above showed a pathetic number *three*. Candice's perfectly manicured, peach-colored thumbnail hovered above the button. The tiny tap would determine the mood for the day, whether she'd admit it or not. *Tap.* The screen changed, and her eyes scanned the notices. *Jim Posted a New Picture, Tammy was Live, Four New Likes.* The total was now twenty-one.

The phone flew with ease out of her hand, the rounded corner of its glitter case breaking through the mauve wall paint and half-inch-thick sheetrock before falling to the floor with a loud smack. Candice shot up in shock; it wasn't the first time she'd thrown the phone, but it was the first time it had broken the wall. Panicking, she turned to see if Sam had seen what happened. She hadn't even realized he wasn't in bed and that the shower was running. *What the hell is going on with me?* Jumping out of bed, she raced to her phone. The wall hadn't hurt it, but the Malibu Blu Italian tile floor that cost more than the home she grew up in had shattered the screen. More tears. Panic fell on her like a wet blanket. Not because of a dent in the wall of their obnoxiously expensive bedroom, nor was it a fear of Sam; it was because she would not have her phone for...*oh God, how long?*

The cover story was easy (spider on the wall), but getting a new phone, well, that certainly was not. The day was filled with stupid child-centered activities she had to attend. If she skipped them to get the phone, she couldn't take pictures of Gunnar at gymnastics, pottery class, or the rec center's newest attempt at riding the pop wave of mindfulness, "Contemplation Time." If she missed any of those, the girls would text her and ask where she was, but even worse, they would post their own pics and *she* wouldn't have any. Candice wouldn't be tagged in anything. Everyone would talk about the day, but not about her. Worst of all, there would be no *likes*. These thoughts ravaged her brain; it was worse than *Sophie's Choice*. Miss all of the classes to get the new phone, or be embarrassed by taking her iPad to take pictures with. Either way, it was a lose-lose.

Not for a split second did any guilt or self-blame seep into her thoughts. After all, it was not her fault she threw the phone; it was the *likes*. If she'd had more than Tina's, Kelly's, or Brittany's posts, she wouldn't have thrown the phone, but they all had over *forty* each. What the hell was she doing wrong? It had to be Gunnar; he just wasn't cute enough anymore. Why did he have to become a preteen? Maybe she needed to have another kid. Babies get a ton of likes no matter what the picture.

The day was turning out to be the worst in history. Her iPad was dead. Not only did it need to charge, it was screaming at her to do an update. She was going to have to wait to check if the likes increased later. Breakfast was a nightmare. Had Gunnar always eaten that way? His mouth hung open, milk drying on both sides of his lips, rainbow flecks of cereal crammed in his teeth and covering his tongue like a confetti bomb had exploded. His hand held a full spoon, dripping milk, frozen in front of his face as he stared at the tablet to watch whatever terrible YouTube video was on. The spoon only entered his mouth once every other minute. In between spoonsful, his tongue lolled back and forth around his lips like it had its own brain and was begging for the food to keep coming. He was a zombie. Sam had his phone out as well, but he ate a bit quicker and with more elegance, as if the years eating before watching devices at the same time had trained him.

As she watched the two of them disappear into their own worlds, she'd never felt envy so strongly. It was infuriating. She was missing so many posts and she couldn't make any comments; everyone was going to wonder where she was. The anxiety this caused was crushing. Candice couldn't imagine wishing this suffering on her worst enemy. *No one should suffer this much.*

As she cleaned up breakfast, still not sure why they couldn't have a housekeeper like Kelly did, a decision was made. *Skip the classes to get the phone.* It would be a blow and she was not sure how to overcome it, but getting a phone back couldn't be more paramount. After seeing Sam off to work and picking out Gunnar's outfit—annoyed he didn't look good in anything—she got dressed and the two of them rushed out to the phone store. Standing in line, she was appalled, not only by how long the wait was, but by the people who were in the store. There were just so many lower-class people there;

they wore t-shirts with stupid slogans, sweatpants, dirty and worn-out shoes, and worst, gaudy gold jewelry. *Who the hell wears gold anymore? Oh, I know, the people who wait in line at the phone store at ten in the morning on Wednesday!* As this thought crossed her mind, she realized something: *It was a perfect post.* People would die laughing! If she took a picture making a cute "disgusted face" with the people behind her, it would get more than seventeen likes. She *needed* a phone *now.*

After cleaning the cheap waiting area seats with a disposable wipe, she sat with Gunnar and waited. Although she estimated that twenty minutes had gone by, she looked at the store clock and realized only four had passed. Having nothing to look at was just cruel and unusual punishment. What the hell did people do in the old days while they waited?

"Gunnar, don't touch the arm," she scolded. "Don't touch anything you don't have to, please." In response, her son looked around for a few seconds, raised his eyebrows, and went back to his YouTube. She hated the videos he watched, not because of the poor quality and asinine content, but because of how many damn views the videos got—tens of thousands, millions, all with nothing more than a kid playing a stupid video game or an idiot parent trying to recreate a kid's movie with store-bought props. It disgusted her. *She* should have that many views.

Candice's attempt at a YouTube page was such an epic failure that she'd paid six thousand dollars to a professional "scrubber" to erase all traces of her account.

Not only were the four thousand total views on the six videos of the "Candy with Candice" page embarrassing, seventy percent of them were by men thinking the page belonged to a stripper. The comments were beyond cruel and burned into her brain forever. Thankfully, the scrubber did his job well and the only humiliation was when a friend asked if she planned on doing any more videos. They all knew she wasn't going to and that it was a sore subject they were not supposed to bring up. They did it just to push her buttons, just like they always rubbed in her face how many likes and shares their own pages got. *Belly breaths.* Calming down, her name was called.

Leaving Gunnar in his comatose stare, Candice approached the tech at the counter with a big smile, wanting to make sure things went as smoothly as possible after all. "Hi, I broke my phone today," she said with a puppy dog whine, hoping the young, dark-skinned, dark-haired, dangerously good-looking man would take pity on her and bring her a new phone as soon as possible.

As she set the phone down on the counter, the man sucked in air quickly. "Broke is an understatement. They won't be able to fix that. Do you have the insurance?"

Candice laughed. She wanted to explain that her husband thought phone insurance was a scam, but that would be wasting time. She needed a phone as soon as possible. "No, I just want to get a new one and make sure this one is wiped clean."

The man nodded, turned to walk away, but then hesitated. "Ma'am, may I ask what you mostly use your phone for?"

Candice made a face. "It's a phone. I use it for…phone stuff."

The man laughed politely and smoothed his yellow polo. It was only then that she noticed he was not wearing a nametag. "I have to plug it in to clean everything off the phone. I'll need you to scan your thumb, but don't worry, I can only see analytical data on my screen. No pictures or emails or anything like that."

There was a standard white phone cord sticking out of a small hole in the desktop, but the man ignored that and reached under the counter to reveal a thick brown wire covered in what looked like deer fur. Candice scrunched up her face. She had seen different novelty cords before, but that one was just gross. As the man plugged the end of the furry cable into her phone, Candice glimpsed a brilliant flash of light. It was so jarring that she let out a small gasp and looked around the store to determine from where it had come, but no one seemed to have noticed anything. She shook her head and dismissed it as a migraine flash.

"Your thumb, ma'am." The good-looking man had to ask twice before she realized what he meant. Curiously, it looked as if fur from the cord was now starting to grow around the phone.

She placed a thumb onto the small cracked home screen. The shock of pain felt like a needle shooting into her finger. She yelped, pulled back, and saw the blood on her thumb. "Shit, broken glass." Popping the thumb into her mouth, she looked at the man. He was not smiling; he was simply looking at the computer screen with a dead stare. "Don't worry, I'm fine," she mumbled under her breath.

After a solid thirty seconds of silence from the man, a smile started to cross his face, small at first, then bigger and bigger, to the point where it was almost impossibly big. Dread was starting to set into Candice's stomach, but she could not understand why it was there or what was going on. "Ma'am, according to your screen time usage, you spent nine hours of your day yesterday on social media."

Candice felt her face get hot. Her brain turned and turned as she tried to think of a way to respond. Just as she decided on a "how dare you" response, the man spoke again. "I have good news for you. I can see how important these apps are to you. We are only allowed to give out one of these a month as a top-secret test, but if you are interested, I can offer you a new phone called the Di-Go Social. We say it like the name *Diego*. It does all the stuff an iPhone does, but it is created specifically for social media."

Candice thought it sounded interesting, but it also sounded like a scam. "No, I just want the new iPhone. It was time to upgrade anyway."

The man's smile faded. "Seventeen *likes*, Candice. You are going to tolerate that and those other bitches always getting more likes?"

It felt like a punch in the gut. How on earth could

he have known? Was the phone recording her this morning? She couldn't think of how to respond.

The man continued. "Have you seen that talentless teen girl on TikTok, the one with over sixty million followers, tens of millions more than every celebrity there is? Well, she has the Di-Go; she was one of the first to get it. She'd still be popping pimples in the high school's bathroom if it weren't for this phone. Instead, she is on every late-night talk show and is one of the most famous people in the world right now." Candice felt a bit dizzy. She had never heard of this phone, but for some reason she trusted this man, or at least she wanted to.

The man reached under the counter and pulled out the most beautiful black box she had ever seen. It was clean and smooth, its cover a soft black material with nothing but a pair of antlers stamped in shiny black foil. "How much is that going to cost me?" Candice heard herself say through a fog.

The man removed the lid to reveal a stunning phone that made her old iPhone look like a brick. He picked up the box, turned it over, and let the phone drop into his hand. Adjusting his grip, he held the device up to Candice. Sleek black antlers were on the shiny back of the phone, and just under the logo were the letters *Di-Go*. As she stared at them in awe, he said, "Smile." Caught off guard, Candice didn't even look at the camera, let alone smile. "Perfect," he responded with his own smile.

"Delete that right now!" Candice demanded, but

when he turned to show her the picture, it was magic, plain and simple. She hadn't smiled, yet the picture of her showed a smile so elegant it made her jaw drop. In fact, it was the best picture she had ever seen of herself. "How—"

The man smiled again, held up one finger, and typed on the phone. "Look at this." It hadn't been more than five seconds from when he last tapped the phone, yet the picture was up on Facebook and the *likes* were coming in so fast, she lost her breath.

"I'll give you anything for it."

Within thirty minutes of getting in her car, Candice made four different posts, all selfies with lame quotes.

New phone, first selfie!

Need coffee!

Taking the day off with my Gunnar. God, I love this kid!

Love driving with the windows down. ;)

By the time she parked at home, all the pictures had over a thousand *likes* each, more than she'd ever accrued on a single picture. The girls were going to shit themselves; *she'd* be the new leader, not Tina. Candice couldn't believe her luck. The day went from worst ever to the best. And she didn't even have to pay for the phone. The guy just made her promise that she would post as many pics as possible, every day, and not to let anyone know about the phone, as it was still in beta testing. What a deal! *No need for belly breaths.*

By the time dinner rolled around, which was takeout because she didn't have time to cook, Candice had made over twenty posts and all of them were racking up those beautiful, beautiful thumbs-up and hearts over and over. The average picture was hitting three thousand likes. It was better than her wildest dreams. Even Gunnar looked five pounds thinner and like a model in the pictures. The phone had also been blowing up all day. Tina asked if she had gotten a makeover because she looked spectacular, Kelly asked if they could hang out when she never wanted to come over, and Brit, that bitch, accused her of hiring a team of make-up artists and photographers. Candice was the envy of the town; hell, maybe soon she would be the envy of the world. Even Sam noticed her when he came home. Instead of disappearing into his office for the night, he actually wanted to spend time with her. *Thank you, Di-Go!*

When it was time for bed, Sam fell asleep instantly and she stayed on the phone, going through all the comments and responding like a teen girl in love. Before she knew it, it was yet again three in the morning, only this time she hadn't slept a wink. It had been seven hours since her last post and the thumbs were slowing to a drip. She knew this was because it was the middle of the night, but maybe if she did another post, it would get those thumbs popping quicker.

Slipping off her shirt, she adjusted the comforter to ensure just enough cleavage showed, then put on a pouty face and snapped a pic. She looked like a damn vixen. She posted it along with, *Just can't sleep tonight, anyone else?* and instantly started to get likes and more hearts than normal, but also some weird comments.

Stunning, love the antler shadow. Is that a filter? I love that effect! She had to look carefully, but sure enough, there was a subtle outline of antlers above her head. It was odd, but it must have been just the logo reflecting with the flash.

That weekend, Candice and the family went to their cabin for some quality time. Of course, she posted every few minutes and spent at times over thirty minutes getting just the right picture to post. Everyone loved the pics and kept commenting about how amazing of a family they had, that they were so lucky and looked so happy. The comments made Candice ecstatic, even if it was far from the truth.

On Sunday, she had to bribe Gunnar with an ice cream to put down his damn tablet for a picture, and Sam got madder and madder that she would not put the damn phone down. "Can't we do anything without you having to post about it? When are you going to realize that actually enjoying this shit is more important than your friends' comments?" Sam screamed at her more than once and in a variety of ways. They fought more that weekend than they ever had, but it didn't matter. She had her *likes*. On the drive home, Candice announced she was going to turn the guest bedroom into a mini studio to try and become a professional influencer. Sam didn't respond.

A month later, her followers had gone from four hundred to four thousand and her *likes* hit an average of ten thousand a day. Candice truly believed she could become a social media influencer, but then all of a sudden, the *likes* started to slow down. From ten thousand, to a thousand, back down to a hundred a day, all in the course of a week. Her plans were disintegrating right in front of her eyes. The pics still looked amazing. *So, what was it? What was going on? Was the phone broken?* Before the last thought even finished, she had the keys and was racing to the phone store. Candice was halfway there when she realized Gunnar was home alone. For a split second, she thought of rushing home, but she knew this was more important; besides, he wouldn't even notice she was gone, as he was on his tablet. As long as the battery didn't die, she would be fine.

Pushing her way through the line, Candice didn't sign in or even wait a second. She walked right to the counter, to the same good-looking man, only he looked like he had gotten thin. Really thin. It was like he'd lost all the muscle that was piled upon him before. His skin was even a bit lighter, as if he were sick. Seeing her, he smiled a weak smile and asked the old lady who was at his station to give him a moment. "Let me guess…not working as well, right?"

Candice was in a fluster. Her head bobbed like a pigeon's on crack. Fighting back tears, she eked out a simple *yes*.

The man nodded and looked at the back of his hand, a bundle of bones wrapped in dried up tissue paper. *What the hell?* Candice ignored the sight and waited for his answer. After a large sigh, the man simply said, "You're not giving enough."

Candice heard his words, opened her mouth, then

shut it and spoke. "You…you mean, I need to do more." The man nodded slowly. There were a thousand questions running through her head, but she understood and left.

At home, it took twenty minutes to find Gunnar. He was hiding in the master bedroom closet behind a stack of shoes; when she discovered him, he was crying and had wet himself. Candice didn't ask him why he was there; instead, she simply told him to go wash his face, get changed, and use some of Dad's red eyedrops because they had work to do. Five minutes later, Candice was dressed in her best dress, a shiny red mini skirt made of silk that was bought for their last cruise. *She looked killer in it.* After dragging Gunnar into the new studio, she started snapping pictures. Smiling, being silly, jumping in the air, pouring bottles out, dropping things in slow motion, fast motion, different outfits, different lighting, shot after shot after shot. Post after post: *Photo time with my Gunnar! Let's take some photos! Silly faces. We are such dorks!* Every picture was captioned with a different quote. In less than an hour, she had over a hundred posts. She was posting so fast she didn't even have time to check how many likes she'd gotten. Gunnar, thankfully, was too scared to complain or not obey her constant demands.

At the start of the second hour, Gunnar did something he didn't do much: he spoke. "Mom, I'm tired. Can we stop? Please." There was a hitch in his breath and he was fighting back tears.

Candice paused for a second, looked at her phone,

and found she had to stop herself from throwing it: she'd acquired only a thousand likes in the past hour. "No. Wipe your face and put some glasses on. You look like shit. We will never get likes with you looking like that." When he broke down crying, she was done with him. Without thinking, she grabbed a prop bottle of champagne and smacked him upside the head. He dropped to the ground like a duffel bag being thrown off a train. *At least he can't complain now.*

The little shit was heavier than she thought, yet she got him up and into a chair and balanced some sunglasses on him. But he wasn't smiling. It took some work, but using an old metal coat hanger and some tin snips she found in the garage, she was able to make hooks that went around the corners of his cheeks and around the back of his head. When she pulled, it made him smile broader than she ever could have hoped!

She pulled on the wire and made him smile big and snapped some pics. They looked great, though you could see the wires a bit. She could Photoshop them, but she just didn't have time. She had to get another post up! She posted the first set with the hashtag *My Dummy*. People would think he was dressed as a ventriloquist dummy. *It was perfect.* A few seconds later, the likes started to jump up, especially for that picture. So, she pulled on the wire and took even more. More posts. *More likes.*

Posing for another picture, this time with her wearing Sam's dress shirt to make her look like a classic ventriloquist, Candice pulled the wire a bit too hard. The metal ripped right through Gunnar's soft cheeks, splitting both sides wide open like some sadistic child version of the Joker, only without make-up. When the wires pulled back suddenly, Candice fell and kicked over the tripod. As she got up, she saw the blood pour everywhere, just as Gunnar's eyes shot open and he started to scream. She watched in horror as her son's tongue slid between the massive gap on the right side of his mouth that showcased all of his baby teeth and new molars. The blood-covered tongue looked like some alien worm searching a foreign surface. Not knowing what to do, she fumbled on the ground, found the champagne bottle, and hit him again. Gunnar wobbled like a cartoon cat about to faint, then dropped again. *Belly breaths.*

Candice picked up the tripod, the phone still attached, and found that there was a bit of blood on the antlers. After wiping it off, she noticed three letters before the Di that were not there before: W. I. N. These confused her, but there were more pressing issues.

Turning the phone around, her heart slammed when seeing that the screen was flashing one little word: *Live.* Somehow during the scuffle, the live feed button was hit. *Streaming live.* The little thumbs and hearts floated across the screen, one after another. There had to be thousands. Turning the camera around, she smiled and started to talk to her fans. It was like a switch had flicked on. She reached down, dipped two fingers into the blood pooling around Gunnar, and then wiped a streak down her cheek like a teardrop before making a pouty look. More comments; there was so many. *They loved her—truly,*

truly loved her. One word repeated: *More.* They wanted and needed more. Just as she was about to reach down to get more blood, the garage door started to rumble. She turned back to the screen and smiled. "Well, my dears," she said to the adoring audience. "You are in for a treat. We have a special guest coming on our show tonight... What shall I do to him?"

Knowing it would make for some killer footage and rack up millions of views on YouTube, Candice rolled Sam's head down the stairs after the police busted through the doors. She knew the bodycams would film everything and eventually it would make its way online. She had become a legend. When the seven SWAT team members saw the teeth marks all over Sam's face, they all aimed their guns at her and screamed for her not to move. Knowing that someone (Brittany, most likely, that envious bitch) would eventually call the police during the live feed, she had gotten changed for the finale.

When Candice showed up at the top of the staircase, with her freshly done hair covered in silver sparkles, wearing the black dress with the one shoulder strap, her bare skin shining with more sparkles, she looked, in a word, *marvelous.* Placing her right hand gently on the banister, she took a step down, ignoring the officers' commands to stop, and spoke.

"You know how many likes this is going to get, boys?"

Skim

There was just something so damn peaceful about the blue screen gently gliding through the clear water, scooping out the tiny intruders: leaves, bugs, pollen, and the occasional dead mouse or frog. Gail could walk around the edge of the pool for hours just obsessively skimming and skimming. She used to feel stupid about wanting to do a task no one else in her family would do, but then she saw a segment on the news about how in some cultures, in one of those far off countries she would never visit, people would use wooden rakes on sand to find their "zen." In a way, skimming the pool was not much different, only her skimming had a purpose, unlike raking sand for no damn reason.

Every morning at six a.m., before the family was up and the chaos of a normal day began, Gail would go outside in her sixteen-dollar department store pajamas and skim the pool. There was always a lot of stuff mindlessly floating on the surface in the morning, especially if it had been a windy night. She liked those mornings best. The more she was able to scoop out, the more she felt like she had accomplished something. The morning of August 6th was one of those days. The night before, there was a powerful, albeit quick, storm that raced through at three in the morning, stirring up the dog and causing Sid to wake up crying. While she lay in the tiny child-sized bed assuring Sid that "God was just bowling" each time the thunder cracked, all she could think of was how much she was going to have to skim in the morning.

That morning's PJs were the purple ones that had laughing giraffes on them; supposedly, Sid had picked them out, along with a pack of cheap metal earrings, for Mother's Day that year. She hated both presents but wore them dutifully to make Sid happy. When she saw the pattern on the pajamas on Mother's Day, it was hard to force a smile. She despised giraffes, ever since one had licked the side of her face at a zoo when she was on a school field trip. At fourteen, the time of sexual awakening, having a massive black tongue lick her face and fondle her ear in front of all the other horny kids was the start of some intense teasing with a long list of jokes and names she did her best to forget. Ever since then, she hated seeing a giraffe, cartoon or not. But there was no way Sid could know that, so she wore them every Thursday and Friday night without complaint. When she walked out, purple head to toe, giraffes all over her, she was not expecting anything except a nice calm morning of skimming. When she saw the young man sitting with his legs in the water at the far corner by the ladder, her heart slammed so hard she thought the heart attack she knew she would have one day was finally upon her. Half of her family, one quick widow-maker by their fortieth birthday—now it was her turn.

Taking a few solid deep breaths, she assessed her heart; it wasn't stopping, so steadied herself focused on the situation. Gail didn't scream. She didn't cry or run for help or go back inside to get Dave. She simply stared at the man, for he had her skimmer across his lap. He looked about twenty, maybe twenty-two at the oldest; he still had the hard, firm body of a kid who cared what he looked like. His skin was tanned and his muscles were taut; he had stubble on his face, but just in an amount that made it look like he wanted people to know he could grow a beard if he tried. The hair was light, almost sandy blonde, and he was squinting at the water like he was really thinking about it. Once her heart started beating fast but normal again, Gail momentarily thought she was in some sort of wet dream, and that she was going to accuse the man of being in her yard and he'd apologize, saying he must be at the wrong house but that he could "make it up to her." Of course, the music would cue and they'd have steamy sex on a blow-up float at that point. For a brief moment, the thought overtook her, sending a shot of blood to her nipples, making a giraffe's smiling face pop out. Taking a deep breath, she shook the thoughts and cleared her throat.

The man—boy—shook his head as if clearing it, and looked up at her. Seeing his eyes for the first time, she knew she must have known him somehow, but searching the deepest parts of her brain, she could not place the man. Then he smiled, and it was a great smile, one so good that he must know how to use it. He raised his hand and put it out like he wanted a high five, but really, it was some sort of stoic wave. She could see from over fifty feet away that he had rough callouses under each finger on his palm. For some reason, those callouses made the other giraffe pop out. After two seconds of holding it up, he set his hand back down and went back to staring at the pool. Gail looked around the yard. Nothing else was out of place; even the pool gate was closed. Besides, it was always locked; the man would have to have jumped over to get inside, so he couldn't have accidentally shown up as if he were at the wrong house. Suddenly conscious of her braless nipples poking through her pajamas, she crossed her arms and tried to decide what to do, but her brain was having a hard time thinking clearly.

The smartest thing to do would be to go back inside, lock the sliding door, and get Dave to scare the man off before calling the cops. Yet, for some reason, it was the last option on the growing list of thoughts. With one deep breath, she thought of her skimmer and how no one else had ever touched the long cold piece of aluminum she held so dearly each morning. She started to walk. She stayed on the other side of the pool from him, taking each step slowly, making sure he made no sudden moves. Directly across the pool from him, twenty feet away to be exact, she suddenly found herself pulling up her pant legs and sitting down and slipping her bare legs into the chlorinated coolness. The water was colder than when she normally swam, yet it felt absolutely wonderful encircling her toes and ankles, rising up to the back of her calves. Hearing the tiniest of splashes she made, the man looked up at her and smiled that ridiculous smile. It made her feel things she hadn't since high school. It was a feeling she hadn't known she missed.

It was silent for almost two full minutes as they both stared at the water—that is, the man stared while she snuck glances at him every few seconds, wondering what she could say while at the same time not wanting to ruin this moment she was enjoying so damn much. In the end, she didn't have to do anything. The man stood up; amazingly, he used no hands but simply leaned, pulled up one leg, and balanced effortlessly on the other leg; it seemed utterly impossible to Gail. His legs still dripping, he walked over to the fence and placed the skimmer on its hanger, before gently brushing off his hands. Gail's heart started to speed up, asking her what the hell was going on. As the man approached her, it lost its rhythm and made her start to hyperventilate. Ten feet away, five, then right next to her, he stopped. She knew she should scream, but she just didn't want to.

Leaning down, he reached out, placed his hand ever so gently under her chin, turned her face towards his, and spoke. "See you tomorrow, beautiful?" Gail's mouth opened ever so slightly, but nothing came out, not even air. The man smiled that damn smile again, let go of her face, and walked away. She knew that smile…those eyes.

Gail was in such shock, she couldn't even turn to watch him leave, even though she desperately wanted to see how he got out. After a few seconds of stoicism, Gail felt a wave of pin pricks firing across her body; it was a rush of pure excitement and joy so pure, she started to cry as the fence rattled behind her. She assumed he had jumped over, then her mind started to race. Who was he? Why was he there? Where were his shirt and shoes? Why was he coming back? And the loudest of them all: How could he find her beautiful all dumpy in her cheap pajamas? With the thoughts firing through her mind, she got up, retrieved the skimmer from its hook, gently slid her hands over where his had been just a moment earlier, and smiled. It was just a damn skimmer, but knowing he had touched it made it feel different. With her heart fluttering, she skimmed and skimmed with something she was not use to lately: a smile.

It was hard to think the rest of the day. She made her normal breakfast, and did her daily routines of games and activities with Sid: playtime, park, walk, snacks and the like. On the outside, it looked like a normal day. On the inside, it was nothing but thoughts of the mysterious man and the obsession over whether she had dreamed the encounter or if it was real. The security cameras only focused on the entrances and exits of the house; there was not one on the pool. However, at the exact time he left, she could hear the fence rattle on the back-door camera footage, so he had to be real. More than once, she had to stop herself from being in a daze, looking off into the distance, and ignoring Sid. It was the most exciting thing that had happened to her since her son was born. She didn't want to admit to herself that the man was even more exciting than seeing her own child take his first steps.

While the thoughts ping-ponged through her head all day, she never let them race to a sexual fantasy, even if the thoughts were trying to bust through the back of her mind like a horde of zombies through cheap plywood. Even though she didn't let the thoughts in, her body still felt tingles, her nipples kept getting erect, and she was more aroused down there than she had been in years. She felt a slight bit of guilt, but who would blame her? Dave had looked at her and treated her differently since Sid was born. Their once-a-week roll in the sheets was now down to once every few months, and only if she got a few drinks in him and wore something sexy. The thought of Dave, her husband, no longer wanting her made her feel like shit, so she locked it away with the zombie horde and focused on who the hell the man could be and why was he coming back…if he really was.

Sleeping that night was torture, plain and simple. Gail would be surprised if she got more than ten minutes of sleep in total. She was just so excited. Even worse, she felt a nagging guilt for shaving her legs and trimming down there, for trying to figure out what was the least "Mommy" pair of pajamas she had, and for wearing a rejuvenating mask to sleep. It was like she was getting ready for a date back in her dorm room, only she didn't have cheap nip bottles hiding under her bed and her old roommates to giggle with. It was all ridiculous. She should have just told her husband so he could be up in the morning and confront the kid when he showed up.

All night, she thought about waking him up in the morning and having him go down with her. At times, she nodded her head and told herself that was the plan, but she knew it wasn't. All of her thoughts were just that, thoughts, and she knew she wouldn't do anything with this kid either. What the hell was she thinking? She'd go out in her own backyard while her family slept and sleep with someone who was almost half her age, who she didn't know, all while wearing her animal print pajamas? What an idiot.

At five-fifteen, earlier than she ever woke up, she was wide awake and ready to head outside, but she calmed herself and slowly went to the bathroom to "freshen up." On a normal day, she would never have done that before skimming. At five-thirty, she walked down the stairs, her heart slamming. She was hoping to arrive before the kid did so that she could see him arrive, if he came at all, but when she got to the sliding door and looked out, he was already there, shirtless and wearing jean shorts and no shoes, just like the day before. This time, though, he was standing and skimming the pool, doing her job. Gail couldn't breathe. There was just something about this boy that was so beautiful; she wanted him in her arms desperately...but this time, it was not even sexual. She just wanted to feel him, to hold him and feel he was real. Without thinking, she exhaled and opened the door.

Today she had on a pajama set of shorts and shirt that was light pink with little green flowers and yellow ducks. It was still cheesy and not flattering, but it was the best pair she had, one she could wear to get the mail if she had to. Stepping outside, she suddenly felt a boost of confidence as she walked along the pool. She was surprised that the boy didn't even look up or acknowledge her in any way. He was on the short end of the pool, next to the diving board, scooping up a burnt orange leaf that had changed color and fallen much too early. When she stopped at the corner, she took a deep breath and spoke. "You came back."

She carefully watched him as a small smile came across his face and he nodded once, so gently it could almost be mistaken as no movement at all, yet he did not look at her or speak. Standing there, feeling exposed with no bra on and in her pajamas, she crossed her arms and watched as he lifted the skimmer out of the pool, gently passing the mesh basket in front of her and then over the fence before he turned it upside down and let the leaf fall out. It fluttered too gently for being water-logged. When it hit the ground, the man sighed heavily, turned back to the pool, and looked at it as if upset before he set the skimmer back on the rack. Gail watched as he swallowed, once, twice, three times. He seemed to be getting more and more upset with each swallow.

"Are…are you alright?" Gail asked with hesitation as she took a step towards him, nervous but also concerned. His head snapped back and water started shooting out of his mouth, his body convulsing like he was having a massive seizure. His hands shot up and grabbed at his throat, clawing at it up and down. Gail started to panic. She was going to scream for help, but realizing that it made no sense for water to be shooting out of his mouth, she froze fearfully in place. How could a mental breakdown seem so damn real? Gail started taking slow steps backwards, telling herself she was imagining things, but then the boy fell into the water with an enormous splash, covering her in droplets of all-too-real chlorine-scented water. Feeling the coldness soak her shorts and legs shocked her into reality: if it were only in her mind, she wouldn't be wet.

The kid looked strong. If she jumped in after him, he might pull her down. Racing to the fence, she grabbed the skimmer and lunged it towards him to offer some sort of help. He was thrashing, struggling, gasping, spitting out water. It was awful, but when he saw the skimmer in front of him, he stopped moving and started treading water gently. Water oozed out of his nose and he took a small breath before looking Gail right in the eyes. Then that smile, that damn smile, crossed his face.

"See you tomorrow, beautiful." With two strong strokes, he was at the edge of the pool, pulling himself out. Before she could find words, he had hopped over the fence and was striding off down the yard towards the endless back woods, soaking wet, with no shirt and no shoes. When he was out of sight, Gail collapsed onto the cement, shredding the skin of her knees. Sobbing, she watched a small trickle of blood mix with the pool water as she tried to get a hold of herself.

An hour later, after cleaning her wounds with peroxide and putting some silly neon-colored kids' bandage on them, she rehearsed the story she was going to tell her husband. She tripped and fell: That stupid crack, we have to fix it! Understanding she was losing her mind was another story. It was the only answer and it was terrifying. He couldn't have been real, even if she saw him, felt the water, and heard the sounds. Even if the camera audio caught some distant gurgling, the splash and fence noise, it couldn't be real. No human could manifest gallons of water out of his throat like that and then walk away with a smile. If he hadn't done that, maybe, just maybe, he would be real. Unlike the day before where she was giddy and curious, she was now terrified and doing her best to not think about how she might be losing her mind.

Throughout the day, Sid asked her in his cute, high-pitched voice, "Why cry, Mama? You sad about me?" on several occasions, which made her cry harder. It was nearly impossible to hold it together as she looked up psychotic breaks, delusions, hysteria, and a whole pile of other mental issues. None of them helped, but a lot scared her. The only calming factor was that she didn't seem to have the other symptoms or factors related to any of the conditions—at least, she didn't think she did. By the time dinner came around, she had gotten herself together enough to pretend nothing was wrong as she listened to Dave drone on and on about his work issues she couldn't care less about.

That night, when it came to sleeping, she was shocked to find herself falling asleep with ease, as she expected to be up all night again, only this time with worry. When she woke with a start at just after six in the morning, she had an idea that excited but scared her. Grabbing her phone off the charger, she went out of her room and down the hall to the only window that had a view of the pool: Sid's room. Sid was still sleeping like a beautiful little doll, so she carefully stepped around the toys and peaked out from the curtain. Sure enough, the man was there; this time, he was sitting on the edge of the diving board, his legs swinging gently back and forth. A hammer slammed into Gail's chest as she lifted up the phone, turned it on, and opened up the video camera. With a trembling finger, she hit record, making sure to keep the man in frame the entire time. When tiny fingers touched her leg, she yelped, dropped the phone, and fell backwards, causing Sid to cry.

After shushing him and telling him gently that Mama was just looking outside to see the weather, the boy calmed down. It was then the idea came to her. Picking up the phone, she clicked on the photos and opened up the video she had just taken. Sure enough, the man was there in the video…but could anyone else see what she saw? Though Sid's eyes were still groggy, Gail pushed PLAY and held the screen up to her son. "What do you see, Sid?"

Sid looked at the video and squinted as if it were some sort of test. Scrunching up his lips, he simply said, "Sid by pool, no go pool by self. No swim alone at night. Dangerous." Gail blinked rapidly. She had no clue why her son called the man Sid or mentioned night, but he clearly, clearly saw the man. She stopped the video and pulled Sid close to her as she smiled and laughed. "Thank you, baby. Thank you."

The next eleven days, the man appeared over and over again. Always wearing the same shorts, no shirt, and no shoes. Some days, he sat on the edge of the pool; others, on the diving board; and during a few, he skimmed the water. No matter what Gail asked him, he never spoke. Mostly, he would ignore her, though occasionally he'd flash her that brilliant smile. Even when she jokingly named him "Pool Boy," which she called him daily, he did not react. When she asked if this was part of some fraternity joke or an elaborate prank, he didn't even smile. No matter how much she prodded and researched the man, she kept his visits completely to herself.

For a few days, she got up early to see where he came from and at what time, but it told her nothing about this mysterious man. Four times she tried to follow him, but every damn time he was able to lose her in the woods, simply vanishing like a magician or some eighties horror movie killer. One day, she flashed him to get a reaction, but it did not faze him one bit. Screaming, pushing him, shaking him, even slapping him did absolutely nothing. It was like he was a robot on autopilot. It was beyond bizarre, but Gail started to find him comforting and looked forward to each morning with him…except the days where he did his choking routine.

Thankfully, it was not every day, but about every three, he would stand completely still and spew the water before falling in and doing the whole fake drowning bit. It was beyond awful having to watch it over and over. By the third time, Gail just lowered her head and hummed to herself so she didn't have to hear the sound of drowning. Of course, no matter what happened each day, he ended their encounter with his pat line, "See you tomorrow, beautiful."

One day, after fourteen in a row, he did not show up. That day, Gail waited so long for him that Dave came out to ask her what was going on and where his breakfast was. She was so distraught that morning that she kept forgetting to do simple things and constantly kept checking the pool to see if he was just late. But he never appeared.

Day after day, he was absent. Before she knew it, September rolled around and her husband put the cover on the pool and her skimmer in the shed for the following summer. The next morning, Gail went out in the crisp morning and stood next to the pool as if saying goodbye to the pool boy, even though he hadn't shown up in almost three weeks. Occasionally, through the fall and winter, she would look out the window, hoping to see her pool boy. When she went shopping and drove around town, she would scan faces, but she never once saw anyone that came even close to resembling him. That December, she invested in a small desk toy: a small box of sand with a rake. She enjoyed it just as much as her skimming.

As the days and weeks went on, she thought of him only occasionally…until the next pool season came around. The first morning after opening the pool, she thought he would show up…but he didn't. Day after day she thought he would be there, but he never showed and she skimmed alone. By mid-summer she had given up hope and didn't even think of him when she went out for her daily routine. Life was normal. Her two weeks of a thrilling oddity were a lost memory that now seemed like a dream that could be skimmed out of her mind like a floating leaf.

Twenty-three years later, Gail was in her early fifties, still wearing crappy animal print pajamas, albeit two sizes bigger. She was almost fifteen years past the time she thought the widow-maker heart attack would take her, though it had taken Dave instead. With Sid living with his fiancée three states over, she was all alone. The pool was too much to take care of anymore, and besides, no one used it, so she had it filled in with dirt the year after Dave passed. The memory of the pool boy was merely a foggy thought that popped up once every few years, but it was so clouded with time that she dismissed it as having been a daydream induced by the stress of raising Sid.

One hot August day, she went into the old crumbling shed to put away the sprinkler she had been running after dinner. As she reached up to put the sprinkler away on the shelf, she lost her balance and knocked into the shelf, catching herself with a laugh and a sigh of relief, though she let out a yelp as something fell behind her. Grabbing her chest, she looked around to see what had caused the scare, and that's when she saw the faded blue handle of her old skimmer. Laughing to herself, she picked it up and ran her fingers along the fine mesh that was now dried and cracked. Thoughts of how much she missed skimming the pool flooded her mind. She really did love that pool and taking care of it on her quiet mornings. As she was about to put it back, the heat becoming oppressive in the tiny wooden room, she looked at her watch. It was August 6th... August 6th. The date was burned into her mind, even if buried behind some dusty boxes of her memory. It was the first day the pool boy came to her.

Breathing heavy and feeling faint, Gail clutched onto the skimmer and tried desperately to picture the boy's face. She could recall how striking his smile was, but she just couldn't see his face. For some twisted reason, all she could see was Sid's face. He had grown up to become a good-looking man with a killer smile himself...just like that pool boy. Shaking her head, feeling the heat getting to her, Gail forced herself out of the shed. Though the air outside was already over ninety, it felt like walking into air conditioning. Taking deep breaths, closing her eyes, and letting the sun beat down on her, she dropped the skimmer and fell to her knees, knowing something beyond horrible was about to happen.

It took a few minutes, but she was able to get up and inside the house where the real cool air was. As she rinsed her face, she accidentally inhaled some water and began to cough. The sudden hacking convulsion sent a flood of memories of the pool boy's awful choking episodes. And that is when it hit her as hard as falling face-first into the water.

The pool boy—the pool boy was Sid.

Her mind wasn't just replacing him in her memory. It was Sid. The boy who visited her every day for fourteen days was her adult son. Without thinking, Gail grabbed her phone and dialed Sid's number. No answer. She dialed again. No answer. His fiancée's number, no answer. Looking at the clock, Gail screamed and screamed. It was 8:14 at night. She felt stupid, but it all made sense in her head. He came to her in August, the eighth month, and stayed for fourteen days. Fourteen. Eight. Eight-fourteen...8:14.

For over an hour straight, Gail called both numbers to no avail, then the police. She implored the cops in the town Sid lived in to do a welfare check, but they would not check on him, as she had last heard from him that morning. When her phone rang right before nine-thirty, she knew before she answered that Sid had drowned taking a night swim. She was certain that his last words were, "See you tomorrow, beautiful" to his fiancée, who always went to bed at seven so that she could get up at four to be at the news station she worked for. As she pushed the answer button, she heard the sobbing on the other end. She swallowed hard and looked at the skimmer on the counter. This was her fault. He'd told her for fourteen days, gave her a twenty-year warning, the toddler version of him even pointed himself out—it couldn't have been clearer. She simply hadn't put the pieces together until it was too late.

The next morning, Gail silently watched the sunrise in the backyard, sitting right in the exact spot where the pool boy, Sid, would have sat if the pool were still there. Sid by pool, Sid by pool. The tiny voice played in her head. Gail turned the skimmer over and over in her hands just as she heard wet footsteps walking up behind her. She knew he would come one last time to say goodbye.

The Tracks

The endless stretch of steel, held in place by giant slabs of ancient wood and covered with jagged stones, was simply beautiful, especially when a smear of fresh blood was streaked down the long stretch of tracks. The track used to feed her routinely: drunks, workers, daring children, and of course, the occasional suicide that wanted to look like an accident. There were even a few murders over the years. The early part of the nineteenth century was especially bountiful; a stock market crash and the great train collision created a feast. However, as time crawled by, she ate less and less. The humans got distracted by things that kept them inside. More planes flew above than trains ran by, and she grew hungrier every year.

By the late 1990s, the whispers of her existence that used to scare away most, but which also brought the daring to her, faded away. Children no longer played alone out in the woods, and especially not by the tracks. As parents were no longer worried about a train running over their unsupervised little ones, they didn't have to spread the stories about the monster that liked to grab children who played by the tracks and throw them in front of trains. At one point, every child believed. Teens and adults, on the other hand, thought it was an urban legend...until they suddenly couldn't move or felt an unseen force throw them onto the tracks as a train barreled down on them. Now, no one believed. Only a handful of old-timers had vague memories of her story.

***

"Senior photos cost how much?" Clarice's mother balked before throwing the small pamphlet in the trash. "I'll take them myself; you don't need some fancy photographer who thinks they are a damn artist. Seriously. Over half a grand to take a handful of photos!" At seventeen, Clarice knew to let her mother rant. There was no point in stopping her or arguing, even if she was dead wrong, so the girl sat there with a glazed look on her face as her mother, who was starting to look like a drunk *Saturday Night Live* character, rambled on.

"Watch this." Her mother picked up her phone, took five pictures of Clarice, flipped the phone around, and showed the screen to her daughter. Clarice didn't want to look at them; she *hated* pictures of herself. Hell, she hated mirrors, too. All she saw was the muffin top spilling over her jeans or the ever-present acne that showed through her layer of foundation. The idea of taking senior pictures was terrifying, but she was going to do them for Eve. She had promised her.

"If I had the right lighting, I could shoot it, I swear. They make movies on these things now. And for the price of one, you should be able to. Wait, I think one of my old sorority sisters does photos," her mother said to herself before she looked at her phone. Clarice knew it was her chance to get away, so she quietly stood up and slinked to her bedroom.

With her door shut, she spoke out loud to the air, telling the small hockey puck next to her bed to play music. Within seconds, a mix of her favorite songs came on. Opening her phone to scroll through TikTok—her favorite hobby, one she could do mindlessly for hours—she gasped. The unflattering picture her mother took was on the screen. With lightning speed, her thumb tapped the photo and deleted it. After a few seconds, she went into her deleted folder and deleted it from there as well, making damn sure the photo would never see the light of day.

Before opening TikTok again, she texted Eve and told her about the drama, hoping the girl she loved would tell her it was alright, that she didn't have to get pictures done. Instead, Eve replied:

I know she probably acted cray cray, but your Moms is right. We will figure it out.

Clarice's stomach dropped. She hated when her mom was right, but she also hated the idea of having to take these stupid photos.

K.

It was all she could muster for a response. She was depressed now and wanted to wallow in it. With an overly dramatic sigh, she resumed her TikTok wandering and didn't move until three hours later when dinner was ready.

***

The last time she ate was over two years ago. She was getting weaker and the world seemed to be fading away as she slept more than she didn't. Sleeping meant that if someone did come near, she might not be able to get them, but almost no one came anymore, so it didn't matter. The fight she had left was little and weak. If she never woke from one of her slumbers, then so be it.

The fight she'd had once left her many years ago when the steady supply of food slowed to a trickle. For decades she fought against the unseen force that kept her from getting further than twenty yards away from the track. Sure, she could travel the length of the track, for hundreds of miles, but she could only follow it where the tracks led. If the rail split, she could only follow it the way the switch was positioned. When she got to the railyards on either end of her lines, she could go no further. Thankfully, the lines seemed to go forever, but traveling them on an empty stomach was nearly impossible, which is why she settled to a comfortable stretch near a bridge where there was plenty of shelter.

When she slept, her stomach would ache with hunger so much that she would dream of the times when entire trains would derail, serving her a feast that would keep her filled for months. The last one like that was well over a hundred years ago, a head-on collision. One-hundred and one died; it was the greatest meal of her life. So much pain, so many souls, so much food. Now…now she was lucky to get a possum or raccoon to snack on, but she couldn't survive on their meat.

They did not hold pain inside them the way the humans did.

***

Clarice walked down the drab beige hallway, clutching her books to her chest, her face turned down like always, just hoping to make it to class without any human interactions. *One more year, one more year,* she thought to herself as she passed the other students laughing and goofing off next to blue dented lockers. The few classes she had to walk alone to, without Eve, were pure torture. They made her stomach knot up, and more than once she had to slip into a bathroom stall to catch her breath and stop herself from crying. She'd always wait until the bell rang and then rush to her class where she would receive a dirty look from her teacher and a late notice alert on her phone a few moments later. The detentions she received from those piled up tardies were worth avoiding the sea of "normal."

She sat in math class that day, her stomach pushing into the edge of the hard desk, which always left a red welt by the time she left for home. They did not make the desks for students over two hundred pounds. She stared at the clock, watching the thin red stick tick around the circle. If she focused hard enough and counted the seconds in her head, the class seemed to go by quicker. Unfortunately, on this day, there was group work, which meant she could not ignore everyone. She was going to be forced to move her desk into a group of four and "work together" for half an hour to solve a stupid equation she could do in four seconds in her head.

It was just her luck that she got pushed together with the three catty girls who had tortured her for years. One of them once threw a handful of dog shit at her in the seventh grade, making for the most humiliating experience of her life that resulted in her being called "Shithead" for the following two years. Clarice thought of asking to go to the nurse, but she had done so twice already that week and was warned not to again unless it was an emergency.

The gossiping girls treated her like she was completely invisible, except for the one comment, "Clare, you are good at math, why don't you just work on the problem for us." They'd grown up with her, yet still couldn't get her name right. Clarice felt her face get hot as she pulled out a pencil and started to write out the numbers to avoid looking at them. Her stomach tightened as the three talked about senior photos and how amazing they were going to look. They were spending thousands on make-up artists. They couldn't wait to make fun of everyone else's photos.

Clarice felt faint.

***

Looking up at the sky, she knew that her days were almost over. Everything seemed foggy in her field of vision. She couldn't keep down the last small rodent she tried to eat. It was just a matter of days before she slipped away, ending over two hundred years of existence. While she had awareness and mild thoughts, they never strayed far from getting food. Over the last few decades, she was able to consume some of the humans' world through a magical square device that showed images and told her stories. She was only able to see it from a distance, but there were several places where she could push to the edge of her confinement and see into one of the places the humans used for shelter.

Though she was never able to get close enough to hear exactly what noises the images made, music, on the other hand, was a glorious treat. The workers on the rail used to sing songs as they laid the lines and repaired them, but as time went on, they played boxes that created such wonderful sounds. These days, she could hear music occasionally leaking out from a passing train or a car, but those were only brief flashes, and she would try to hold onto them in her head and repeat. Humans were horrible beings and she despised every last one of them for confining her to these rails and making her eat the scraps the speeding train provided her with. But the music they created was something special that she only assumed their God must have bequeathed on them. Part of her wished she could listen to one full song again. It would be a beautiful way to stop existing: just closing her eyes and listening.

***

The days before the photo shoot, Clarice felt herself becoming anxious and cranky with anyone and everyone. Her stomach hurt a bit more as the days counted down. No matter what anxiety-relieving "tools" or advice from her online therapist she followed, she simply could not relax. *It was a damn picture, so what?* She tried to repeat this over and over in her mind, but the mantra didn't work.

It wasn't just any picture. It was the picture that would freeze time; all three-hundred and thirty-two of her classmates would forever have this picture in their yearbook. *This* one picture would be how she would be remembered best. And the one that Sid, Toni, and Molly would make fun of. Christ, they would probably draw pictures on it and take photos to post online making fun of the "pimpled dyke cow." When those thoughts came into her mind, anger and revenge exploded inside of her like a backdraft. These moments made her understand how some people snapped and did awful things.

When the day finally arrived, Eve placed her soft, small hands on Clarice's cheeks, looked her dead in the eyes, and told her that no matter what, she would love her and the picture. Clarice cried and did her best to hold onto that love to get her through the day.

Her mother had hired the old college friend who'd minored in photography. Clarice had to admit that the woman's photos were great, even if she only took them as a hobby. At least the quality wouldn't be embarrassing. The location they picked was a bit odd—the rickety train tracks by the old green bridge—but she could understand that the depth of field would look really cool and "outdoor" shots were "in" at the moment.

***

Time was no longer a concept; she didn't even know if it was day or night anymore, for she didn't bother to open her eyes. She only slept and thought and slept, hoping for the hunger pains to end and for the powers that trapped her there to finally let her go. She had done her time. Then, as the hunger rumbled and the sleep turned fitful, she heard a voice. This stirred her mind, making her open her eyes for the first time in…weeks, maybe months? The sun was blinding. The light seared her vision, making anger rise in her, and then there were more voices. These glorious sounds gave her a jolt of energy she had not felt in years. Food was near, food was possible again. And it sounded like much more than one person. Could a feast be on its way?

As she crawled out of her hiding spot under the bridge, her limbs creaked and ached with stiffness, which made her fear she would not be quick enough. But after a few stretches and a hissing yawn, she felt ready to pounce and make one last attempt at survival. Her mind had to quickly do some calculations. The train only went by three times a day now, unlike in the old days when one went by every twenty minutes. She used to know the exact second the train would be coming—it was ingrained in her bones— but now…now she wasn't sure. She had to touch the track.

Climbing to the edge, peering from behind a dry shrub, she saw an entire group of women. Three young girls dressed in bizarre and bright clothing. There was also a small group of older people next to the track setting up something. There were eight of them: a full feast, even if she just got the four on the tracks.

Sliding over to the bridge, she slithered her way to the tracks and set a hand on her old friend, the cold steel rail. With a simple touch, she knew the train was four minutes and twenty seconds away; she still had it in her. The excitement was starting to pump hard through her as her stomach jumped up and down with anticipation. Food! Just as she was about to slide up behind the girls on the track, she heard more voices, this time, from the other side of the tracks.

More people were coming. It was going to be a glorious day.

***

Wearing more make-up than she had ever worn, Clarice felt like a plastic doll as she walked through the long field. She and Eve were mostly silent on the ten-minute walk, but her mother and the photographer went on and on about the old days. The constant patter helped distract her from the nerves. What was helping her was the understanding that it wasn't taking the pictures that was hard—that part was easy, in fact—it was seeing them afterwards that she was afraid of. When she told this to Eve, her girlfriend thought for a moment and then said she would look at them first and pick her favorites, because if she loved them, Clarice was *not* allowed to hate them. This deal was easing the tension a bit, but the nerves were still there.

Through a clearing in the trees, Clarice could see the green beams of the bridge. She had always seen it in the distance from the road, but she had never seen it up close, and something about it made her rather curious. Her only concept of train tracks was from movies, especially *Stand by Me*. Breaking through the clearing, she was excited to get a glimpse of the site, but what she saw was like an anxiety A-bomb exploding. There, right on the tracks, right where she was going to take pictures, were Sid, Toni, and Molly in their expensive clothes, an entourage sitting by their side. Clarice stopped in her tracks, but her mother and the photographer walked right by them, laughing at how their "idea must be good if other girls are doing it."

Clarice couldn't breathe; she couldn't speak or even think. All she could concentrate on was Eve's hand holding hers. Trying to suck in some air, she looked towards the bridge and saw something she didn't understand. There, crawling along the tracks, was a giant creature. It had long dark legs: six, maybe more. It had a vaguely human face, but it was stretched and distorted like someone tried to erase it. Oddest of all, it wore what looked like a dress from the Old West. It was white and ruffled, but filthy and torn. She must have been losing it; seeing the girls who tortured her for so many years must have made her mind snap.

She closed her eyes, rubbed them furiously, and looked back. The creature was getting closer to the girls. She wanted to scream, she wanted to yell out, but at the same time, it was *them*. She could hear Eve talking to her, but she couldn't make out the words. She was so transfixed, she started to walk, then run, towards the track, and that is when everything froze…everything except for her and the thing.

***

The anticipation of eating was glorious. Crawling along the track, she felt all of her old talents coming back to her, her body fighting for one more last meal. When she opened her mouth to emit her call, she almost started to cry. She was really going to eat again. The low hum she had not heard in so long came out of her belly as if she did it every day…and it still worked. Everyone froze. They couldn't hear, they couldn't see, they didn't know anything that was happening. All she had to do now was keep them in the trance for—hand on the rail—one minute and ten more seconds, and she would eat.

It was then she saw the movement on her side.

A girl, a beautiful girl, like her, just like her, *was moving at completely normal speed, and she was staring right at her. It wasn't possible. No human had seen her since they'd cursed her to the tracks. Yet, she was staring right at her, coming towards her. Within seconds, the girl was standing next to the track, looking her in the face. She wanted to close her mouth, to speak to the girl, but if she did, the food on the tracks would hear the coming train and move out of the way. She needed them to stay in place or she wouldn't eat. So, she simply stared at her.*

***

The thing on the tracks was magnificent and it was looking right at her. Their eyes connected and Clarice felt a warmth come over her that she had never felt outside of Eve's gaze. They locked eyes, and while they didn't speak, there was a connection between them that made a tear fall down her face. After a few seconds, Clarice heard the train and knew what was going to happen. She knew this poor thing was hungry. She wanted it to eat. She wanted to watch her.

Clarice wanted to help her *keep* eating.

The train, a sleek silver express passenger train rolling at over a hundred miles an hour, flew over the bridge and right at Sid, Toni, Molly, and the photographer. At the last second, the thing gracefully leapt to the side like a jumping spider and landed right next to Clarice a millisecond before all four of them were obliterated on the tracks. As the screaming and screech of the brakes started, Clarice felt warmth in her hands.

Looking to the right, she saw Eve clutching her hand and burying her face in her shoulder. When she looked to the left, she saw a leathery claw-like hand in hers. It was warm and felt nice there. Looking up into the monster's blurred face, Clarice smiled and spoke.

"Dinner is served."

The Child's Photo

I was seven, maybe eight, when I was standing at the checkout counter with my dad at the local grocery store. I wanted a Twix bar. Even though I was already being made fun of for my size by the other boys in school, I always wanted sweets. Candy always won over the shame for some reason. Even though I knew my dad was embarrassed of my size and told me to wear my shirt when I went swimming the week before, I still asked him for the candy bar. Holding up the shiny pack in my hand, putting on my best "pretty please" smile, I heard the bleep, bleep, bleep as each item was scanned, hoping the next beep would be my treat. Dad, wearing his beloved jean jacket in ninety-degree weather, looked down at me with no expression. After a few seconds, he reached up and scratched his massive auburn beard and said, "Come here, Kevin." I put down the bar knowing I was not going to get it; I just knew he was going to whisper in my ear about not wanting me to be the fat kid. Instead, he pulled out his wallet. It was dark black leather and cracked with age. It always sat by our front door in the bowl with his keys; every time I looked at it, the wallet always screamed "Dad" to me. At first, I got excited thinking I was going to be given money, but instead he pulled out a photograph that fit neatly behind the bills, with the fingers carefully covering the back of the photo.

He looked at it for a second, then he looked around—there was no one in line behind us and the cashier was busy scanning. Satisfied, he leaned over, flipped the picture around, and showed it to me.

The piss filtered through my red gym shorts and ran down my bare legs until it hit my tube socks, which did the best they could to soak it up. I couldn't speak. I was terrified and in shock, and on top of it all, embarrassed. The piss that wasn't absorbed by my socks filtered into my high-tops and seeped out onto the floor. My father put the picture back in his wallet, pulled out a wad of cash, and said, "Clean up at checkout number four!" It was followed by a laugh and a fake apology about how his son must have been holding it too long. A few seconds later, the awkward girl doing the scanning looked at me, made a disgusted face, sighed, and then spoke into the metal microphone next to her cash register.

"Marty, a kid peed at checkout. Grab the mop." This announcement made every person in the various lines turn and look at me. My dad looked around, shrugged his shoulders, and then handed over the cash.

A few minutes later, I was sitting on plastic shopping bags in my dad's truck so I didn't "get piss on his upholstery." Over forty years later, the memory of that embarrassment I felt in that moment still makes my cheeks flush, but what I recall most about that day was the photograph. It was the first time my dad used that faded photo to…well, to scare or control me, I guess. The picture…it gave me nightmares, it made me feel sick, and obviously it made me piss my pants the first time I saw it…and the second time.

The photo was of a little boy, about the same age I was at the time—seven, maybe eight, nine at the oldest. He was lying on what looked like black pebbles on a rocky beach. There were some spots of sand between the shiny wet rocks; a wave must have just receded as there were tiny foam bubbles in the crevasses. The kid's dark hair was also wet and stuck to his forehead. Tiny speckles of water covered his entire body and his orange bathing suit that had a blue waistband. The last detail I can give before my stomach starts to knot is that the boy had a small temporary tattoo on the back of his right hand. It was rather washed away; only a faint outline and specs of color remained. Every time I was shown the photo, I forced myself to stare at the tattoo and try to think about what it was to distract myself. After several years, I realized it was a purple gorilla with a small green hat.

As for the rest of the photo, it was awful. Every inch of the boy's skin was bloated with spidery purple and blue lines running all over. The flesh looked so gooey that I used to have nightmares of grabbing his arm and having my fingers pop through the skin, only to pull back my hand in terror to watch his flesh slough off and stick to my fingers. I probably had this nightmare because of the boy's stomach. It was bloated and misshapen, like someone took a soaking wet towel, put it in a paper bag, and then crumbled it all up, letting the paper melt away from the inside—only this bag was torn open, just to the left of his outie belly button, which looked eerily similar to my own. There was no blood, no guts spilling out, just a black hole that looked as if an animal had chewed it open and enjoyed whatever was inside. While that empty gaping hole also gave me nightmares, ones where I would wake and feel my own stomach to make sure I didn't have an open cavity of my own, it was the face that scared me the most.

The boy's face, which was positioned towards the camera as if he were looking into the lens, was blank and empty. With the face being so misshapen and veiny, it was beyond generic; there wasn't a single mole or distinguishing feature. He could have been one of a million boys. Hell, he could have been me, even though it was his eyes that made the piss run down my leg. One was milky white; not a lick of color, not a hint of an iris or pupil, absolutely nothing. The other one, while also milky and featureless, was protruding from its socket, bulging a good two inches outside as if it were trying to escape, yet the tiny eyelids held onto it for dear life, as if they were begging it to stay for just a bit longer. There was nothing else in the photo, as the image cut off right above the boy's knees and the entire frame was filled by the child's body and the pebbles around it. It could have been any beach in the world, any little boy. The photo was so lacking in information that I could never tell if the boy was murdered or simply got swept away and washed up days later. I saw it so many times that if I were ever asked to give a sketch artist details, he would create an identical rendering.

***

Looking back now, I can track my life and growth through how I thought of that photo. In my childhood, it was simply one hundred percent fear. Every time I saw my dad reach around to his back pocket, my knees would get weak, tears would well in my eyes, I would feel sick, and I'd have to consciously hold my bladder. When I would ask questions or plead not to see it, my father was stoic and silent. He would only hold the photo and point at it until my eyes rested long enough for him to be satisfied.

When I was eleven, my balls dropped a bit and I finally asked, "Why the fuck do you show this to me?" It was one of the only times in my life that my father was violent with me. He may have raised his voice and threatened before and after that time, but he never once touched me like he did that day. The second I finished the question, he grabbed me by the throat, slammed me against the wall, and thrust his left knee into my crotch so hard my gut ached for a week.

"You ever ask a fucking thing about him again and you will be just as dead as him, I swear to God." When I woke up some time later after being choked unconscious, I knew he meant it. I never breathed another word about it until I was an adult.

By the age of fourteen, while I wouldn't ask questions, I was full of myself and was no longer scared of the photo. I made a point to show no fear or concern when I saw the dead kid. I would do my best to be tough and I would look my dad in the eyes for a good three seconds before settling my gaze on the photo, making a point that it no longer affected me in the way he wanted it to. By my late teens, Dad only showed me the picture about once a year, though this time it wasn't to scare or to control me; for some reason, he seemed to want me to just remember he had the damn thing, as if forgetting it was dangerous. He would randomly call me to his den, sit me down, pull out his wallet, and tell me to look at it for five minutes. He would set it on the ottoman, tell me to not touch it, hit the clicker of his stopwatch, and sit and watch me. If I looked away, he would pause his old metal watch and stare at me until I looked back down.

It was the early nineties by then and the internet was just being birthed when we got a Gateway computer. After every one of those little sit-downs, I would rush to the computer and search "dead child 1970s," "dead child on beach," and other keywords. I even searched "beaches with black rocks" and every variation of *child, dead, rocks* and *beach* imaginable. The search engine, *Ask Jeeves,* was in its infancy and a far cry from today's capabilities. All the results I got were either irrelevant or traumatized me more. Of course, the curiosity would fade and I would forget all about the photo a few days later until it was brought back out again in another six months, where we would do the whole process over again.

When I moved out of the house, Dad no longer tried to show me the picture. I tried to ask about it a few times, man to man, and eventually, father to father, but every time I asked, my dad looked at me with the same rage he had on the day he choked me unconscious. He balled his fists, looked me in the eyes, gritted his teeth, and said, "*Don't.*" One time, I asked when he was in his sixties, arthritis ravaging his body and twisting his hands into useless knots. I could have knocked him down with one finger, but he was still my dad; he was still the boss and I respected him too damn much, so I shut up and changed the topic to the weather, one of his favorite things to talk about as he got older.

The last time I asked, I was helping him pack to move into a senior living home as he could no longer take care of a full house and yard. He felt defeated but I was still proud of him for making it to his mid-seventies and still mowing his yard. At the end of the day, he handed me a "cold one" and looked around the empty kitchen with a tear in his eye. It was hard for me as well, as it was the house I grew up in. Even though it was just him and me in that house all those years, we still had a lot of memories within these walls. I leaned against the wall and drank from my can as Dad turned and reached into the cabinet to get his favorite beer glass (that he didn't put away for this occasion). I had so many memories of him drinking out of that one damn glass with his initials etched on it; never once did he drink beer out of anything else. As he stood with his back to me, pouring the golden liquid into the glass, I noticed the worn lines in his jeans where his wallet always sat. Without even thinking I asked to his back, "Dad, why did you always show me that picture?" He slowed his movements, grabbed the glass by the rim with his twisted fingers, and turned around. There was no table or chairs left to sit at, so he leaned against the counter and looked at the beer can in one hand, the glass in the other.

"Your mother gave me this glass on our third anniversary. That anniversary is glass or crystal or some shit. Your mom loved stuff like that, making sure to always get the appropriately themed anniversary gift." He smiled, looked at the glass, and then let it fall out of his hands as if it were a handful of dirt he was dropping back to the earth. I jumped to grab it but was too far away. The liquid sloshed over the edges and splashed on the floor a millisecond before the glass shattered. My first thought went to the kids stepping on it and needing to yell for them to not come in—fatherly instincts are like that—but I wasn't home, and the kids weren't here. Stopping myself, I stood above the shards and looked at my dad, his eyes were glossy.

"I fucking miss her," he whispered, staring at the shards on the floor. Mom died before I was even three, four decades earlier, yet he still missed her. The pain I saw on his face made my heart ache and the "what if" start to seep into my mind, a game I played my whole life: *what if I grew up with a mother?* But I stopped myself when I realized that Dad was distracting me and it worked like a charm.

"The picture, Dad…why?" He licked his lips, shook the gloss out of his stare, and looked back up to me.

"Because I had to. Now pick this shit up." With

that, he walked out of the house, into the moving truck, and sipped the little beer that was left in the can as I cleaned up the glass and liquid. I never got to ask again, as my Dad died a week later before he could even fully unpack. While it was ruled an "accident"—an old man falling in a new place he was unfamiliar with, with lots of boxes in the way—I knew he did it on purpose. Leaving the house, having me pack it with him, but not unpacking was his gift to me; his life was now all packed up and put away so I didn't have to clean out his house alone. I could never prove that he fell on purpose, and I kept the theory to myself—what was the point of telling anyone?—but I was positive. It was a gut feeling. Where the box was that he tripped on, the way he just happened to fall and hit his head on the table that was pushed a bit too close, his accidentally taking an extra blood thinner that day—it didn't make sense. It was almost as if he knew he couldn't keep the secret of the photo any longer, so it was better to die with it than tell his reasoning.

***

A few days after, before the funeral, I picked up my dad's effects from the coroner: his wedding ring, which he hadn't taken off in the forty-two years after Mom's death, his Italian horn necklace he always wore, and... his wallet. His clothing was thrown away due to the dried blood. Sitting in my car, I looked at the plastic bag. If I were in some sappy movie, I'd pick it up, take out the ring or necklace, hold it to the light, and sob as the emotional loss finally hit me. That didn't happen, as I was still in the anger phase of my grief and all I could think about was that damn picture. Part of me knew it had to be in there, but the other part couldn't fathom that he would have kept it in his wallet all those years. It had to have been over twenty since I had last seen it.

Nerves pulsed through me like static electricity that wouldn't stop, so I drove around town first, not wanting to go home. I got a cheeseburger I wasn't hungry for at a drive-thru and ate in my car staring at the wallet in the bag. I got out, threw the trash away, and stretched. I drove over and looked at the new high school being built in town; it was coming along nicely, though I got a pang of sadness that my kids would be going to a different building than I did in just a few years. Finally, I parked down by the river walk and looked at the clock. If I took any longer, my wife would be calling and wondering where I was. With a sigh, I grabbed the bag, pulled out the wallet, unfolded it, and spread its tired and aged leather sides wide open. I couldn't help but feel like I was invading Dad's privacy. Looking into its gaping mouth, I could see an array of bills (Dad's "walking around" money) and what looked like a photograph right behind them. *Son of a bitch.* It wasn't until that moment that I realized all the times I had seen the picture, I had never once held or even touched it. The thought of actually holding the item that haunted my entire life made my stomach flip so hard I worried the burger would come up.

Shaking like a junkie jonesing for a hit, my thumb

and forefinger grasped the edges of the worn-down photo and pulled it out so slowly you would have thought I was defusing a bomb. I actually laughed out loud at myself for being so stupid. I had seen the picture so many damn times it was burned in my memory. What the hell did I think would happen by touching it? As the photo creeped up, I let out a long breath, not realizing I had been holding it. Staring at the dead child, the shaking started to settle and my gut slowed its flipping. It was the same picture. No magic spell was released and I didn't burst into flames by touching it. It was simply the same damn picture that was going to haunt me the rest of my life, only now I would never know the reasons why it was used as a tool of torture and discipline. Then I realized for the first time that I had never seen the *back* of the photo. In all those years, my dad had been so careful to only show me the front. How I just realized that in the moment, I have no clue, but looking back, he clearly always cupped his fingers around the back or placed it so I could only see the front. Why would he do that?

The shaking and flips started again, but this time I didn't let them control me. I twisted the photo around and saw the back for the first time ever…and promptly opened my door to vomit up the burger I wasn't hungry for. With my stomach empty, I wiped my mouth, then focused on breathing for a solid three minutes before I thought of the writing on the back.

Kevin Rick Russo
Died 7/11/77
RIP

There, in my dad's neat handwriting, was *my name* and *birthday*. My brain fractured with a lack of understanding, then it shattered into a thousand pieces like a bullet flying through a glass.

Anger boiled in me like I had never felt before. It raged through me, wanting out; it wanted to tear up the photo and punch my steering wheel before ripping it off, but just as I started to scream, my phone rang. The uppity tones of a dance song I could never remember the name of, which my daughter programmed into my phone as her ringtone, paused the oncoming explosion in me. Gasping for air, I set the photo down and picked up my phone. It was a pointless call, like always—just a simple, "Hey Dad, could you get me some sparkling water on your way home? *Thanks, love you, bye.*" The rage oozed out of my pores and what was left turned to sobs that lasted longer than any I ever had.

Looking at the photo harder, I finally saw that it looked like me, but that was impossible. I had absolutely no understanding of what the photo was or why my Dad had used the photo the way he did, but now I had to add another mystery to the pile: why my information was on the back. Dad's actions were sick, perverse—*because I had to*—and left more questions than they answered, but now the photo was mine…and I knew I had to show my children when I got home.

A Happy Story

"Marvin, would it kill you to write a happy story for once?" Marvin sighed and ignored his mother. It was always the same questions when he came and visited. Every Saturday he would stop by, and she would hug him and tell him he was getting fat before sitting down in the living room to chat. She would then fire off the same five questions: *How is your girlfriend? How is the new house? How is your father? How are your feet holding up?* Then it would turn to the question about his writing. He was used to the other questions. He could handle them, and would answer: *She's good. It's a lot of work, but great. Same old Dad. And, feet are fine, Mother* (even though he never understood her obsession with foot health). It was the questions that made him uncomfortable for some reason. Especially because she liked to pause before asking them; those few seconds of silence were always so uncomfortable. Marvin thought of the pause as her engine warming up to yell at him full blast.

"I saw you had a new story come out…but I didn't read it. You know I can't read such horrible things. Why can't you write a happy story?" His mom, with her short hair curled tight and still smelling of the perm chemicals, said without taking in a breath, as if she had to get it all out quickly. Marvin took in a deep breath so deep it was like he was breathing for her as well.

"I don't write happy stories, Mom. You know that." At this point she would always throw her hands up and rock a bit faster in the rocker she hardly left.

"Why can't you be like Nicholas Sparks? He writes nice stories, happy ones."

"People die in his stories too, Ma." She sarcastically laughed at that comment.

"Yeah, but they usually end up happy. Not one of your stories ever ends happy. That is why I stopped reading them: I get depressed." Marvin crossed his arms and looked out the window trying to not fight with her.

"You know I'm so proud that you are a writer, but I never tell my friends what you write because they would be appalled! They probably wouldn't even talk to me anymore if they found out about the filth you write." He couldn't hold it in anymore; she hit the spot that always made him fight back.

"Come on, Mom! I write horror. It's what the readers want. I'm published; I make a living of it, for crying out loud. Do you have any clue how many writers can make a full time living off just writing? It…it's like, less than five percent. I've done damn well for myself. It's nothing to be ashamed of." He checked his watch; it had only been ten minutes since he arrived. If he left any sooner than an hour, she would be insulted.

"Well, for once, can't you just write a happy story…for me? You know my birthday is coming up soon," she said in a cooing voice he remembered from childhood. He took his time replying as he thought about how he couldn't take another Sunday having this argument. He was a writer—he could write anything, right? Why not just give her what she wanted so she could leave him alone?

"Fine, fine! I will write you a happy story for your birthday, but I doubt my agent will be able to sell it." Marvin didn't like the idea of writing a happy story, but it was worth seeing how happy his mom got and her face light up so bright. He couldn't recall the last time he had seen her smile so big.

"I'm so excited; I can't wait to show the girls. See, I knew it wouldn't kill you!"

The next day, at his writing desk in the basement of his house, Marvin looked at the posters of his books around him. *Death to All* by Marx Donavon, *When We Die* by Marx Donavon, *She's Dead* by Marx Donavon. Smiling, his eyes lingered a bit on the name. It still made him sad having a pen name, but like his agent said, Marvin was just not a scary or serious name. Maybe he could use his real name if this happy story turned out to be any good? Using that along with his mom's smile as his motivation, Marvin cracked his knuckles, straightened his back, and set his fingers on the keyboard. *Happy, happy, happy*, he thought over and over again. Nothing came. *Puppies, flowers, hearts*. Still, nothing came. Not one single thought.

Sitting back, he took a deep breath. Story ideas were usually his strongpoint. He had countless concepts stored away in files on his computer, but not one of them would be happy. Why was it so hard for him to think of a happy story? Why? Was his life that miserable? He knew it wasn't. It was perfect. He had a house, a great girlfriend, and an actual paying career as an author. He was never abused as a child, and he never had any great loss except his grandparents, but that was natural. So why couldn't he ever write anything happy?

This thinking session lasted longer than he thought it ever would. The tiny bit of light that came in from the small basement window had faded. Sitting in the dark near the cold, crumbly walls, he realized that might be the problem. He wrote in the basement, purposely keeping it cold, dank, and dirty to keep his mind in a dark place as he wrote. Change the setting and he should be able to change the mood. Grabbing his laptop, he raced upstairs and plopped himself down in the lavender-painted living room his girlfriend had recently redecorated. It was bright, pretty, and feminine. This should do the trick.

After getting comfortable, Marvin was excited; he was ready to write. Hell, maybe instead of a sweet short story for his mother he would write an entire new novel, a romance. He would use his real name. He'd get a new fanbase of women and double his income with a new avenue. Maybe his mother was onto something. Relaxing, he took one deep breath, placed his hands on the keys, and typed... *The woman was beautiful.* His fingers typed fast and furiously, but when they hit that first period, they suddenly stopped. He established that there was a beautiful woman, but then what? Normally he would go on to talk about how her family died and they were coming back as zombies or how she was kidnapped and being held by a sadistic killer. He couldn't do that here. What would a beautiful woman do then?

His fingers left the keyboard to rest on his head. He stared at a photo his girlfriend hung up; it was a field of purple flowers. Women loved flowers; they should inspire him. *Happy, happy, happy!* He repeated it again and again. Nothing came. Frustrated, he typed again. *The woman was beautiful. The axe that smacked between her eyes ended that beauty. The End.* "Happy, Mother!" he yelled out to the room. Frustrated, he got up, paced, and realized he was hungry. Time to make a snack. Maybe with some food in his stomach he could become a bit more sensitive.

With a bowl of black olives, a can of soda, and a bag of chips, Marvin sat back down and munched away. Usually, he never let himself snack while he wrote. It was a disciplinary thing; food was a reward for finishing. This was a new venture, though; his rules did not apply to this story. And it seemed to work, too—the food was making him a bit calmer. Maybe it was just hunger that was ruining his concentration. *Happy, happy, happy*, he thought with a mouthful of olives mashing together with chips. With a swig of soda, he picked the laptop back up. *Flowers, flowers, a florist...who falls in love with...a blind man who can only smell them. As she describes what each flower looks like to him, they fall in love.* It was perfect; this room did the trick. Laughing to himself, he couldn't believe he was ready to finally write a happy story. Mother was going to be so proud.

Marvin's fingers tap-danced across the keys, only

stopping to pop the occasional chip or olive in his mouth. He kept smiling and laughing as he created a world for the unloved florist. Being able to feel this good while writing never occurred to him. Usually he was in a dark, miserable mood to match his characters when he wrote. This was much more enjoyable. So much so he decided to go to Mother's when he finished to let her read it early, and to thank her for opening his eyes. Laughing to himself, he tossed an olive in his mouth and took a deep breath of joy, which was cut short as the olive was sucked into the back of his throat.

Marvin coughed; the little bastard didn't come out. He tried to clear his throat; it was still stuck. Panic did not set in yet, but concern was rapidly falling on him. Calmly as he could, he stood up and bent over to try and use gravity. Three loud hacks later, he realized the olive was making no plans to leave his throat. Panic had arrived. With the lack of air starting to get to him, he could feel his face get hot as he tried to think what you are supposed to do in this situation. Cross your arms and put your hands on your throat! Marvin did this only to realize that he wasted five seconds to do the international signal for choking to an empty room. A chair! That was the answer. *Thrust your stomach on a hard edge and it will shoot right out.* He had seen that happen in numerous movies.

Fumbling toward the recliner, he rammed his breadbox on the top corner, only to have the chair move six inches. Three more attempts did nothing but rearrange the furniture. He had to get to the kitchen to use the counter. Turning, he saw bright spots dancing with black ones all around his eyes. The black ones looked ominously like olives. He took a step towards the kitchen, but it felt as if his leg sunk into the carpet. As he fell flat on his face, he hoped the impact would knock the evil olive from his throat. No such luck. Using the last of his air supply, he sat up, his head drooping. His computer was right there in front of him on the coffee table, right next to the rest of the olives which now looked like spike balls. Marvin could barely see anymore, but he was able to find the right keys by touch to type his dying words. Slowly and painfully, he typed:

Yes, Mother, it would kill me to write a happy story.

About the Author

Michael Gore, the son of a butcher who grew up playing in puddles of blood in his father's shop, became a writer at a young age to cope the murder of his twin sister. With his fascination with death, Michael became a mortician in the early 2000s. He never released any of his writing until one day he was caught slipping a short story he wrote into the coffin of an elderly man about to buried. The man who caught him, encouraged him to publish the stories. The next year Michael released *Tales from a Mortician*, a collection of horror short stories. A few years later, he released his second collection, *Skeletons in the Attic*. Gore is set to release *Halloween Tales* and two more unnamed collection in the coming years. After being released from prison, for a crime he adamantly denies doing, Michael is contemplating his next career as he is no longer allowed to be a mortician. Regardless of his career path, he plans to continue writing until he is no longer legally allowed to do so.

www.ingramcontent.com/pod-product-compliance
Lightning Source LLC
Chambersburg PA
CBHW030307200626
46816CB00002BA/801